SWEET LAVVY

AMANDA GALE

CONTENTS

CHAPTER 1

There is a little cemetery on a remote isle in Maine, an alcove in the trees that line a narrow, winding road. One comes upon it suddenly, perhaps with surprise, as there is nothing else around, not even a church—nothing, unless you count the forests, which are alive with chirping and scurrying and all manner of animal mischief. The trees themselves appear to stand guard—wise, silent observers of the never-ending cycle of life—witnesses who have watched generations pass before them.

The cemetery is as old as the town itself, and all the descendants of those buried there are deceased—all except one, but we will return to him in a moment. As for the rest, many of the gravestones have succumbed to the elements; the forces of nature have eroded the engravings, forever obliterating the identities of the people buried beneath. Other gravestones denote Revolutionary War and Civil War heroes, and their families. But most of the residents were fishermen, humble, hearty, and hard-working.

It may surprise you to hear that it's a cheerful place, especially in the summertime, when the sun filters through the trees and floods the alcove with light. When meandering about, one ponders the connections between the people buried here, though their lifetimes span so many decades. The uneven spaces between the graves are overgrown with wildflowers. The lush green foliage of the surrounding forest makes one think of life among the dead. In winter, sunlight sparkles on ice-covered branches, and as one walks among the graves, a pristine blanket of snow crunches beneath one's feet. The trees now appear draped in white finery, and one is invited to imagine magical things frolicking in the depths of the forest.

It is a winter morning on which our story begins, a brisk day in December, when Nick visited his father.

I mentioned that one resident of the cemetery had living family. It had come to be that Nick bought the house a mile down the road, by the open fields where the street grew wider and straighter as it led into town, and that when his father passed away, he had him buried there so he might visit him whenever he liked. On the morning in question, he trudged forward steadily in the quiet road where the snow had been cleared, his hands in his pockets, his scarf wrapped around his neck and chin, and his breath white puffs in the frozen air.

He was deep inside his thoughts, as he always was on his walks to the cemetery, until he came upon the alcove in the trees. It was then that he looked upward, only to stop short, startled. He had visited this cemetery countless times, and he had never come across another person. And yet, on this day, another man stood before a grave, his silver head bent, looking soberly downward.

"Oh," Nick said. He looked briefly around, but saw no car; he wondered how the old man had come here. "Hello," he added quickly, covering for his surprise.

The other man was older, and his clothes were older, too. He wore brown slacks, and a brown and beige plaid jacket beneath his coat. In his gloved hands, held respectfully before his waist, was a well-worn brown cap.

The man in brown raised his hand and saluted with his cap. "Hello," he replied. He lowered his hand and held his cap in front of his waist once more. He indicated the grave before him with a nod of his head. "This here's my great-grandmother."

Nick momentarily walked past his father's grave, nodding in greeting as he went, and approached the man in brown.

The man took a step to the side to give Nick room to see.

"Lavinia Lockett Sewall," Nick read. "November 12th, 1836 to December 21st, 1900." He slid his hands into his pockets. "She died on December 21st." He looked at the man in brown. "That's today."

The other man nodded. "As you said."

"Did you come here because she died on this day? Or is it just a coincidence?"

"No, son, it's not a coincidence. I'm here on purpose today."

Nick said nothing in response, but turned back to the grave. A couple of cardinals darted between the trees, flashes of red in a field of white. He watched them as they disappeared into the woods.

"How about you, son?" asked the man in brown. "Who are you here to see?"

"My father."

"I'm sorry. You loved him a great deal?"

"Yes," said Nick. "I did."

"You visit him a lot, do you?"

"A couple of times a week." Nick glanced back toward the road, indicating the direction from which he'd come. "I live right down the street. I sometimes walk up here before work. It's a nice way to start my day."

"And what is it that you do for work?"

"I'm a carpenter. My father was a carpenter, too. I learned from him."

"You have a family of your own?"

"Yes, a wife and two kids. A little boy and a little girl."

"Ah," said the man in brown. "Good for you. They make you happy, do they?"

"Yes," said Nick, smiling now, and meeting the other man's gaze. "Very."

The other man's face turned solemn. He sighed and returned his attention to the grave. "That's good," he said. "A man needs a family to love and take care of."

"I've always thought so."

They stood in silence a few more moments.

"You go ahead and see your father. I won't keep you. Thank you for watching over Lavinia with me."

Nick frowned, remembering that he hadn't seen any cars. "How will you get home? You can't possibly—"

"Don't you worry about me, son," the man in brown said, reassuring him with a smile. "I'll find my way."

Nick shook his head. "I can't let you walk in all this snow. It isn't right. I'll call my wife, and she can bring up the car."

"That's kind of you, but no. I don't want any help. Someone is coming for me."

Worried, but desirous to be respectful of the old man's wishes, Nick smiled and nodded. Glancing over his shoulder, he turned and stepped toward his father's grave. After some time, he wished the man good day, waved, and walked home, puzzling over the strange old man in the cemetery.

THAT EVENING NICK sat in his town's tavern, a red-painted cedar-sided little dive at the bottom of Main Street. As it was a cold, snowy week-night, he was the only customer, and the elderly owner sat dozing on a stool behind the bar as a TV screen flashed a sports game above him. Nick sat at a corner table, growing impatient. He had been sitting here for about twenty minutes, staring at the dark wood-paneled walls and neon signs, waiting for his unpredictable brother-in-law Vince. Vince was always late, and Nick would much rather have been in his cozy house with his pretty wife and cheerful children. He anxiously tapped his foot a few times on the floor. He and Vince ran a contracting business together, and he was meeting Vince to break the news that he had decided to take another job. Making the decision had been unbearably difficult, as he hated to abandon Vince, and the job would require him to be away from his family while he traveled. But the substantial pay raise meant he'd be in a better position to provide for his family. He wondered where Vince was, and grew alternately annoyed and amused. He shook his head. This was so like him.

He pulled his wallet from his pocket to withdraw payment for his single beer, ready to head into the crispness of the night so he could go home. Before opening the wallet, he glanced up at the bar. His back straightened, and his eyes widened.

The man in brown, from the cemetery, was sitting at the bar.

Nick blinked. He hadn't noticed him sitting there only moments before. He frowned and eyed his beer: he hadn't had that much to drink, had he?

He was still staring when the man in brown swiveled on his bar stool and spotted him. He smiled, slid from his stool, and headed toward the corner table. Nick politely returned his smile, relieved to know for certain he had made it home from the cemetery. But inside, he was disheartened. It had been a long day, and he wanted to return home to his wife. He hadn't really even wanted to be here when he was meeting Vince; he certainly didn't want to stick around only to make small talk with a stranger.

"It's the dutiful son," said the man as he approached. "My, my, does the world work in mysterious ways."

"Hello again." Nick's smile warmed as the old gentleman grew near. He had a kind face, this man in brown, and he must have been lonely. Nick settled once again in his seat. "Are you just arriving? I didn't see you come in."

The man in brown chuckled. "I have a rather inconspicuous appearance." He glanced at Nick's hand, which was holding his wallet, and his smile drew downward. "Are you just leaving?"

"I was," said Nick, returning his wallet to his back pocket, resigned once more to waiting for Vince, "but I can stay a little while."

The man pulled out the opposite chair and sat. "Thank you, son," he said. "You're keeping an old man company on a cold winter's night."

Nick smiled. "My father used to call me 'son.' No one's called me that in a long time."

"You have a picture of him? Of your father?"

Nick took his phone in his hands and scrolled through his photos. Having found what he was looking for, he held it out for the other man to see.

"This is an older picture. From before he got sick."

"Ah, what a nice-looking pair," said the man in brown, leaning forward and examining it carefully. His eyes darted upward, and his expression turned sly. "You look just like him."

Indeed, he did. Both Nick and his father were tall, with strong, lean frames. They had blond hair, thick and nearly too long as it fell over the sides of their faces, which had rugged, angular features. Their eyes were earnest, and the clearest blue. The two men looked nearly identical, except for the difference in their ages; also, while the father's face was sharper and more serious, Nick's face wore a relaxed, gentle smile.

Nick took back his phone and scrolled to another photo, then held out his hand again. He was feeling a little sorry for the man in brown; there was no reason he couldn't put off going home for a while to keep him company. At least he had a family to go home to. "And here are my wife and kids."

The man's face warmed, and for a moment Nick thought he caught the glimmer of tears in his eyes. The man doted over the photo, his eyes darting between the three smiling faces. He leaned back once more.

"Thank you, son. They're beautiful, really beautiful. Much happiness to you."

"Thank you," said Nick, touched by the sincerity of these words.

The man in brown dabbed his eyes a little with his handkerchief. "Forgive me," he said. "I always grow weepy at the sight of a happy family."

Nick's eyes crinkled kindly as he waited for him to compose himself.

The man tossed his finger upward, indicating the room. "This town hasn't changed much since the last time I was here. Though this tavern is new."

"Not really," said Nick. "Jack's been running this place for about thirty years, I think."

"My family's ties to the isle go back to when it was founded. We have lots of stories about this town. But the most interesting story of all is Lavinia's."

"What makes her story so interesting?"

"Ah, well. It's your classic ghost story, a mystery. No one at the time *knew what to make of it. It's a rather strange story, though a romantic one."*

Nick was intrigued. "I'd love to hear it, if you've got the time."

"Oh, I've got plenty of time," said the man in brown. "In fact, time's about the only thing I've got."

June, 1856

LAVINIA TRAIPSED through the brambles toward the light. In the woods, a canopy of branches made the forest floor dark and cold, but ahead she saw the gravestones, awash in sunshine. Her eyes on her destination, she picked her knees up higher as the land sloped upward, breathing heavily and clutching more tightly to her daisies, their white heads bobbing with her movements. In her haste to return in time for dinner, she stumbled from the forest and into the cemetery, tripping on a tree root and tumbling to the ground. The daisies fell from her hand and scattered on the leaf-strewn cemetery floor.

"Oh, bother," she muttered, reaching for her daisies, then startled when two shoes appeared in her field of vision.

The shoes were followed by knees, then thighs. Lavinia lifted her gaze and gasped at the sight of the pleasant face before her.

"Mr. Sewall," she said, straightening her dress and bringing her hands to her long black hair, which, parted strictly down the middle and pinned into a chignon, had loosened during her brisk walk from town. She pressed the wispy black strands back into place. He was crouched before her, his nose mere inches from hers. Her heartbeat, already healthy from the exertion of her walk, picked up speed.

"Allow me, Miss Lockett," the dark-haired young man said,

and gathered the fallen flowers. Having collected them into a neat, floppy pile, he handed them to her, his blue eyes kind beneath his cap. "There you are, now. Good as new."

Lavinia took the flowers and began to stand. As she did, the young man took her hand to pull her up. They faced each other by the edge of the gravestones, Lavinia blushing as she held her flowers, the young man holding his jacket, which was slung over his shoulder.

"Are you all right, there?" he asked. "That was quite a tumble."

"Oh, I'm all right. I'm so clumsy, I tumble all the time. It's rather ridiculous."

"Well, there I'd disagree."

"And what would you call it?"

"Well, Miss, I think I'd call it adorable."

Lavinia's lips parted, and the thumping of her heart renewed.

"Oh, I'm sorry, Miss," he said, his face turning solemn. "That was rather forward of me."

Lavinia was speechless, breathless from her fall and from his unexpected compliment. "That's all right," she replied, a little shakily.

"You've torn your dress," he said, pointing toward her calf.

"Oh, dear," she said, bending downward and sticking her finger through a large gash in the indigo skirt of her day dress. She straightened the skirt and smoothed down the fabric over her corseted waist, then rearranged her shawl around her wide bishop sleeves, pulling it tighter over the swelling of her chest.

"Ah, well," she said. "Nothing that can't be mended."

"Certainly. A little tear's got nothing on you, Miss. You're the best seamstress in town."

"Oh," she said, looking away and blushing. "I'm hardly that. There are many seamstresses more experienced than I am. And I still work by hand. I wish I had one of the new sewing machines. I could do so much more, and save my fingers much soreness."

"I hear you already do fine work. Mrs. Copley next door says you've quite the knack for it."

"Mrs. Copley is very kind."

They said nothing for a moment or two.

"Are you here to see your parents?" he asked.

"I am, yes."

"I'm here to see my mother."

"Yes, I imagined as much."

"Actually, I was just leaving. We had a nice visit."

Lavinia's eyelashes fluttered as she calmed herself, still flustered from nearly falling into Mr. Sewall and growing increasingly weak-kneed in his watchful gaze. She had always thought him handsome. He was dark-haired and blue-eyed, with sharp, chiseled features. He was tall and broad, with a muscular, well-built form, the strength and virility of his figure evident even beneath his cream checked muslin shirt and suspenders, and sable-colored wool trousers. Lavinia could perfectly imagine the straining of his powerful arms and shoulders as he forced the chisel into the granite surface at the quarry, deftly handling the heavy drills that would help split the blocks from the massive stone bed. A slight, waify woman, she was keenly aware of how small she was by comparison, and was mesmerized by his strength. She usually tried to avoid him; his beauty intimidated her, and the intensity of his eyes unsettled her in a way she could not explain. Something in her core stirred at the sight of him, and she was simultaneously drawn to him and frightened by the effect he had on her.

Standing before him now, however, she could not avoid him. She looked about nervously, aware of the impropriety of being alone with him here, but strangely exhilarated by it. She summoned her courage and met his gaze, and made herself speak.

"It's a fine day for a walk," she managed. "Bright and cheerful."

"It is," he agreed eagerly.

"I find summer days so pleasant," she went on. "The air is so sweet. Like honeysuckle."

"Exactly so. And you can enjoy it more today than on any other day."

She looked at him curiously.

"It's the summer solstice, you see," he explained with a smile. "That means it's the longest day of the year, with the shortest night."

"Oh," she said, returning his smile. "How lovely."

"Indeed, it is. The stars and planets have aligned just right. There's something poetic in that, don't you think? Summer solstice is one of my two favorite days of the year."

"What's the other?"

"Winter solstice," he said. "That would be—"

"—the shortest day of the year," she finished triumphantly, "with the longest night."

He grinned, his eyes sparkling and his face glowing. "Exactly right, Miss. Exactly right."

Lavinia pursed her lips to contain her glee, charmed nearly speechless. "How do you know so much about this?" she asked.

"I'm very fond of the stars. I'd be an astronomer if I had my way. In fact, I believe I'd live in the sky, exploring the planets and unseen places. Or I'd sail across the sea, where the stars would surround me, nothing but stars as far as the eye can see."

"You're quite an adventurer."

"Only in my imagination, Miss. Not much adventure to be had here in Dearham."

She was silent, pondering the adventures she'd have if she could do as she pleased. She had never thought about it before.

"The solstice is a good day to visit a cemetery," he went on. "Legend has it that spirit energy is strong on the solstice. It's supposed to be the bridge between journeys of this life and the next."

"Do you believe that's true?" she asked skeptically, eyebrows raised.

"No, I suppose I don't," he said, his voice cheerful and his hands in his pockets, rocking back and forth in a boyish manner. "But I've got no evidence that it isn't."

"Would you like it to be true?"

His mouth set as he appeared to think about it. Then he smiled. "Yes, I think I would. I think there's poetry in that, too."

"You like poetry." She returned his smile. "I like it, too, though I haven't read much of it."

"Well, that's all right, Miss. Poetry's not just on the page. It's something you sense in the air, something you feel deep down inside yourself." His smile gentled further. "That's why poets write it to begin with."

Lavinia was enchanted. It seemed he was as amiable as he was handsome. She regretted that she didn't have more time.

"Thank you for saving my flowers," she said. "I suppose I should deliver them."

"Of course. My apologies. I shouldn't keep you."

"Apologies aren't necessary," she replied, unable to suppress a small smile. "It was delightful seeing you."

"And you, as well. I wonder if..."

He faltered, studying her, and she raised her eyebrows with anticipation.

"I wonder if I might call on you. To see you again. So we might continue our conversation at our leisure." His face flushed, and he smiled awkwardly. "But I'd understand if you declined, Miss Lockett. In fact, there's no need to answer at all."

"I would like that very much," she blurted before she could stop herself, fearful that he would grow too nervous and change his mind.

He smiled widely in triumph, now standing tall. He nodded. "All right, then. I will. Thank you, Miss Lockett."

"Please, call me Lavinia. Lavvy, even, if you'd like." She blushed more deeply, aware of her boldness, and feeling a little thrill. "That's what I'm called among my friends and family."

"I thank you again. And I ask that you please call me Theodore."

"Thank you. I will."

Theodore smiled, tipped his hat, and sauntered toward the path in the woods.

Lavinia watched him walk away, feeling restless and hopeful. Then she approached her parents' graves, where she laid the daisies at their feet and sang to them, confided in them, and relayed a message of love from her sister.

CHAPTER 2

"*Her parents had died of the consumption, you see," said the man in brown. "One year previous. Lavinia lived with her sister and brother-in-law and worked as a seamstress to help pay the bills."*

"I take it she was close with her sister."

"Oh, yes. Those girls always loved each other dearly and were practically inseparable even after Isabelle got married. Lavinia's sister Isabelle married a Mr. Lyle Forsythe. He was a manager at the quarry. Nice fellow, a good match for Isabelle."

Nick nodded thoughtfully as he glanced at the clock on the wall. Vince was now obscenely late. He was growing grateful to the man in brown for providing a distraction while he waited. "And Theodore? His mother had passed away, too?"

"A few years before that, yes. He had no brothers or sisters."

"He must have been lonely."

"I think he did all right," said the man in brown, with a smile. "He and his dad, they got along well. Fished together, they did, and played cards with the other men in town. Theodore, he was a happy, cheerful sort, the kind who appreciated what he had."

"And how did he know Lavinia?"

"*Well, it was a small town, as it still is. Their families had lived here for years. They passed each other in town most days, going about their errands. But they hadn't really talked before.*"

"*It seems to me that they had wanted to, though.*" Nick smiled and folded his arms across his chest. "*It sounds like they had noticed each other.*"

"*They had,*" said the man in brown, his eyes warming wistfully. "*I suppose each was too shy to approach the other.*"

"*So did Theodore visit her?*"

"*Yes. Visit her he did.*"

"*And what happened?*"

"*What happened was, they fell in love.*"

"LAVVY," whispered Isabelle, standing in the doorway of Lavinia's tiny bedroom, her wide eyes sparkling. Her arm was wrapped around her little daughter Betsy, who sat comfortably on her hip. "Theodore Sewall is here to see you!"

Lavinia looked up from the gown she was mending and sat back in her chair.

Isabelle gestured with her hand, suggesting her impatience. "Aren't you going to come downstairs?"

"Yes," Lavinia answered, then paused, flabbergasted and speechless. "I'm just surprised. I didn't dare hope he would call on me."

"Well, he said he would, and he did. That can mean only one thing!" Isabelle's face wore a bright smile that made her already cheerful face that much prettier. Betsy began fussing, and Isabelle shushed her. "Just a minute, love. Mama is trying to talk some sense into your auntie!" She turned back to Lavinia. "Don't dawdle, now, Lavvy. Come on downstairs." She hitched Betsy higher on her hip, then put her hand to the side of her face, whispering once more. "Oh Lavvy, he's so handsome!"

Lavinia carefully kept her expression impassive until she heard her sister's footsteps fade; then her hands abandoned the gown, and she folded them in her lap as she attempted to calm herself. Her heart was pounding so quickly her stomach hurt. *Theodore Sewall is in my house*, she said to herself, her insides overturning, *and he is waiting to see me*. She closed her eyes and envisioned his face, imagined him standing in Isabelle's sitting room at that moment. Why was he there? Lavinia daren't hope he harbored feelings for her. Her fondness for him was silly and girlish, based on nothing; she hardly knew him. And yet she couldn't help but wonder what else would have brought him there.

She stood and smoothed down the pleats of her navy blue dress and wide white collar, then stepped before the mirror on her dresser and neatened the pins that held back her hair. Frowning at the pallor of her skin, which looked even paler in contrast with her dark hair, she pinched her cheeks. Then she took a deep breath, smiled, and walked out of her room and into the hallway, the wide wooden planks creaking beneath her feet despite the lightness of her steps.

She placed her hand on the banister and stepped gently down the stairs, peeking around the wall as the sitting room came into view. Her fair sister Isabelle sat in the rocking chair to the left of the hearth, grinning broadly, while Theodore, dressed in camel-colored trousers and brown waistcoat and jacket, with a crimson cravat tied around his neck, sat in a floral upholstered wingback chair to the right. Most unusual, though, was that Betsy was standing before him, watching him and giggling with delight. Lavinia's heart melted as she realized that Theodore was performing a magic trick for the little girl, his smile mischievous as he held Betsy in suspense. He pulled a coin out from behind Betsy's ear, eliciting wild laughter from Betsy and Isabelle alike. Upon hearing her footsteps, he looked up, and his face brightened. He hastily rose.

"Good afternoon," Lavinia said as she approached. "How delightful to see you."

"And you, as well, Miss," said Theodore, with a little bow of his head. "I hope my visit is no intrusion."

"Not in the slightest. I've been mending all morning." She stretched her fingers a bit, noting the soreness. "It's a welcome distraction."

He stood before her, tall and broad, and Lavinia inhaled the hard, dusty scent of the quarry, as well as the cozier scents of wool and firewood. It was an exciting change from the more feminine scents of her sister's house—the cinnamon of their baking, the crispness of new fabric, the laundry soap. She wondered if the scent clung to his skin as it did to his clothes. Would his skin feel rough, or smooth? She looked nervously at Isabelle, certain she could read her mind.

"What a lovely trick that was," she told him, unable to keep from smiling. "I didn't know you were a magician."

"There's magic everywhere," said Theodore, waving his arm in the air. "Isn't that right, Betsy?"

Betsy clapped, laughed, and jumped up and down with glee.

"Mr. Sewall is such a showman!" cried Isabelle. "How did you know just what would calm Betsy?"

"I think it's useful to put oneself in the mind of a child sometimes," said Theodore, with a smile. "Don't you?"

"Absolutely," said Isabelle. She smiled, as well, more thoughtfully.

"Shall we sit?" Lavinia asked, too brightly, the final word culminating with a dramatic upturn. She bit her lip, reproving herself, and took her seat in a forest green chair. Sitting straight, she daintily crossed her ankles and folded her hands on her knees as Theodore and Isabelle reclaimed their seats. Betsy played with a doll by their feet.

"Please excuse the warmth," said Lavinia. "This room grows frightfully sunny midday."

"It's a fine room, light and cheerful," he said, leaning forward, and smiling. He glanced around the little sitting room at the dark floral wallpaper and oak furniture. He gestured toward the wall to their left, where a shelf displayed decorative porcelain plates and vases. Above, two silhouettes hung in black oval frames. "I've been admiring these. They are your parents, no? Mr. and Mrs. Lockett?"

Lavinia nodded, silent as sadness tugged at her heart.

"They were kind people," he said. "I always thought so."

"Thank you, Theodore," Lavinia said softly. "Mr. Sewall," she corrected, conscious of her sister's presence.

Theodore said, "I saw your mother, once, tuck a blanket around the shoulders of Mrs. Leeds on a particularly cold day."

Lavinia offered a sober smile. It sounded just like her mother. Mrs. Leeds was a poor woman who had lost her husband to consumption many years before. She sat on a bench out by the wharf, in all weather, gazing at the sea, and no amount of coaxing could persuade her to go inside.

He continued. "I hear you've been teaching the little Wellington girls to sew, now that their mother has passed." His smile grew tender, the kindness in his eyes in delightful contrast with the hard lines of his face. "I can tell your mother lives on in you."

Lavinia was silent as a flush rose to her skin beneath the bodice of her dress, then crept up over her chest and onto her cheeks. What an odd, delicious feeling this was. She was twenty years old. Other boys had caught her fancy before, but there'd never been this restlessness in her blood. They had never looked at her as he was looking at her now.

"Thank you," she whispered finally, returning his smile.

She watched him a moment longer, their gazes locked. The space between them seemed filled with unsaid words, and she looked away, suddenly bashful.

Betsy bumped her finger on a table and began to cry.

"It's time for your nap, little dear," said Isabelle, rising. "Mr.

Sewall, it's been lovely to see you, but if you will excuse me, I must tend to Betsy."

Theodore rose, his face losing some of its luster. "Of course. I understand." He bowed slightly to Lavinia. "May I call on you again, Miss Lockett?"

"Oh, there's no need for you to leave, Mr. Sewall," said Isabelle. "I trust I can leave you two to continue your conversation."

Lavinia raised her eyebrows, surprised. "You don't object, Isabelle?"

"Not at all," said Isabelle, plucking her daughter from the floor. "Mr. Sewall is a gentleman, and besides, it isn't his fault my daughter needs her nap." She smiled at Lavinia, her gaze lingering a moment longer than necessary, and hurried up the stairs.

Lavinia braved a glance at Theodore, who was watching mother and daughter as they climbed out of sight, clearly as delighted as she was.

"Well," he said when they were alone. "That was quite generous of her."

"It was," said Lavinia, with a crooked grin, vowing silently to thank her sister later.

The two sat once more.

They passed an awkward moment or two in silence. Lavinia looked at the carpet and mindlessly fidgeted with her skirt.

"Miss Lockett—Lavvy," said Theodore, leaning forward and folding his hands on his knees, and her heart skipped a couple of beats at his addressing her by her given name. He looked at her frankly, his blue eyes deep. "In truth, I am glad to have you alone. What I have to say is rather forward, I'm afraid." He paused a moment. "But I am compelled to tell you how happy I was to have met you in the cemetery that day."

Lavinia blushed as something primal stirred in her. She rubbed her lips together to compose herself.

"You were?" she asked. "Why is that?"

"Well, I enjoyed our talk about the solstice," he said. "And I suppose it's also because..." His brow furrowed, and his eyes darted to the side momentarily. He met her gaze once more. "I suppose it's because, you're the prettiest girl in town."

Lavinia straightened and froze. "Oh, Mr. Sewall, I am not!"

"Oh, but you are," he insisted, the words now gushing. He continued, ignoring the incredulous shaking of her head. "At least, you are to me. In fact..." Now he shook his head as color crept over his face. "No, but I shouldn't. It's presumptuous of me."

"You should!" said Lavinia eagerly, abandoning propriety. "Undoubtedly, you should."

"Well, I was going to say," he went on, turning his hat nervously in his fingers, "that you've inspired me to write a poem."

Lavinia stared at him, wide-eyed. She leaned against the back of her chair.

"It's laughable, I know," he said, and laughed himself. "I write the occasional poem. It's not something I often admit. But I thought, in light of our conversation about poetry—"

"May I hear it?" she asked softly. "May I hear the poem?"

He hesitated a moment, then inhaled deeply before reaching into the pocket of his coat until he found what he was looking for. He withdrew a folded piece of paper, opened it carefully, cleared his throat, and read.

"Upon a solstice afternoon,
Among the graves I stood;
The spirits whispered in the wind
And danced within the wood.

"Alone I wandered, on this day,
The longest of the year;
Until, out of the forest, nigh,
Sweet Lavvy did appear.

"Her hair was dark as raven's wing
Or winter's midnight skies;
But sunbeams did illume her smile,
As starlight did her eyes.

"She spoke to me of daisies
And of summer's golden hue.
We celebrated poetry,
And honeysuckle, too.

"A gentler heart, a truer grace,
I surely ne'er did see.
I thank the spirits in the woods
Who led sweet Lavvy to me."

His hands shook as he folded the paper and returned it to his pocket. A furious blush had crept from beneath his cravat and over his neck and jawline, threatening to color his entire face. He glanced tentatively at her.

"So," he said hoarsely, and cleared his throat again. "There you are."

Lavinia struggled to control her breathing. She felt she should have been embarrassed; but rather, his proclamations had made her bold, and as she watched him nervously fold and refold his fingers together, she felt the mad pulsing of her heart must be visible through her dress. She shifted in her seat, her motion pulling her dress tight against the curve of her hips. Theodore's eyes grazed over her on their way to the floor. A wave of heat flooded from her core all the way to her fingertips.

Mistaking her silence for offense, Theodore spoke solemnly, his voice so soft as to be barely audible. "I apologize."

In response, Lavinia reached into the pocket of her dress, where her fingers gripped a folded piece of stationery. His eyes were drawn by her motion, and he watched her with curiosity.

Lavinia's heart now beat furiously. She opened the paper and began to read.

"I came upon him
As he stood
Among the tombs.
And though
We spoke but briefly, still,
The memory looms.

"'Twas on the solstice,
We did meet,
The longest day;
Alive with
Spirit energy,
So he did say.

"The kindness
In his smile
When he helped me stand;
The fire
In my bosom
When I took his hand;

"The passion
In his voice
When he admired the skies;
The gentleness
Illumined by
His starlit eyes—

"I sigh, I swoon,
I hunger,
And e'er changed I be;

One man doth make
My spirit soar,
And it is he!"

When she was through, she looked up to find him leaning forward with his hands clasped on his knees, watching her.

"Why, Lavvy," he said quietly, his lips spreading into a smile. "You write poetry, too."

"No, I don't," she replied, looking back down at the paper with wonder. "Only this once."

His smile grew gentle. "Why this once?"

She said nothing, but her lips parted as they locked eyes.

"It's incredible, isn't it? The likeness?"

She nodded.

"I sure am glad I met you that day," he said. "It seems it was destined to happen."

She nodded again, gravely. "I suppose the stars aligned just right."

LAVINIA AND THEODORE continued to see each other. Theodore called on her frequently, always playing with Betsy and working his way into everyone's hearts. As a result, Isabelle and her husband allowed the two young lovers to converse privately, sit in the garden, and even, eventually, to walk around town together. At night, in their own rooms, by candlelight, they wrote poetry for each other, and read it aloud when they saw each other next.

They strolled up and down the wharf, gazing at the fishing schooners. Fishermen scurried about bringing the fish from below deck, where they had been gutted and salted, and carried them off to be rinsed and salted again, then laid out to dry. The lively sounds of boots pounding on the boardwalk and orders shouted in sailors' vernacular rang through the air. Above the activity, the tall masts stood perpendicular to the docks and jagged shoreline. Behind them were the cedar-sided structures that housed the canneries, packing factory, cooper's shop, and small customs house, where salt was brought from Spain. Beyond peaked the triangular roofs of houses, and beyond that, the tree-topped mountains, softly faded against the sky.

Lavinia watched the water. The waves lapped lightly against the docks but grew stronger out toward the sea. Her eyes drifted to the horizon, to where the fishermen would return before too many sunsets.

Theodore lifted his chin and looked upward at the tall sails with wonder.

"Wouldn't it be an adventure," he said, his hands in his pockets and his eyes sparkling like the waves, "to sail out onto the sea?"

"No, I don't believe it would," said Lavinia, her hands holding her stomach as she imagined a ship at the mercy of the waves.

"Ah, but the stars, Lavvy. Just think of it, just you and the sea and the stars." He folded his arms across his chest. "I've always wanted to go to sea."

"Why didn't you?"

"My mother strongly objected, and I didn't have the heart to oppose her."

Lavinia watched him with admiration. He looked down at her, smiled, and held his arm for her to take.

"What is it about the stars that makes you so fond of them?" she asked, her hand resting cozily on his forearm.

Theodore looked wistfully out to the sea, then indulged in a long, deep breath.

"They're so far away, yet they appear so close. Haven't you ever looked out your window at the stars, and felt you could pluck one from its place in the universe?"

Lavinia had felt this way, yes. She stood beside him, feeling the thick sea breeze in her hair, taking in the salty fragrance of the air.

He said, "You know, some scientists now claim there is star dust in all of us. That the stars aren't as far away from us as we think. They say we're built from the same materials as the heavenly bodies, that we're all one with the universe."

Lavinia thought this was a beautiful idea, though she didn't believe it. It seemed impossible, that something so grand, so unknowable, should be inside her, too.

"The notion appeals to me a great deal," he went on. "It means I can go anywhere, that I'm everywhere. That I'm connected with magical places. That I can do things I can't do here." He paused a moment. "Also, it means everyone who has ever been, is with us still. It means we're connected to all who come after us."

She didn't know about all that; it was a lofty notion, and her head was too full of young love to pay it much heed. She enjoyed a pleasant flip of her heart as he patted her hand with his own, and she smiled with contentedness as she let him dream aloud. She adored his passion for the sky, his interest in science and his desire to be part of the larger universe. She nodded as he described the draw of the sea, but to her it sounded ghastly.

Another day, they picked blueberries at Mrs. Meade's farm, the old red barn resting before the cool green forest. There was something delightfully naughty about munching berries together, about coyly feeding each other the tart, round fruits.

"Isabelle would not be pleased," she managed to sputter, her body still tingling from the feel of his fingers brushing her lip as he rolled a blueberry into her mouth.

"Forgive me, Lavvy," he replied, casting her a sly, crooked grin, "but Isabelle isn't here."

They gathered wildflowers together in the fields on the edge of town, the sun high in the sky and the mountains of Maine nestled lazily in the distance. The air was sweet with summer and the fields vibrant with color. Lavinia hiked her skirts around her lace-up boots as they collected tiger lilies, black-eyed Susans, and asters. Theodore tied a bundle with a string and handed it to her.

"For you, my sweet Lavvy."

Lavinia's heart did somersaults. She took the flowers and held them before her waist.

"You look like a lovely bride," he said.

She looked at him fondly, in his light-colored trousers, linen shirt, and suspenders. The sleeves of his shirt were rolled up to his elbows, revealing strong forearms, and his skin had a healthful tan. He was smiling at her, his blue eyes kind and his lips pulled tight.

The rapid fluttering of her heart made her feel pleasantly dazed. "Do I?" she asked shyly as he took her hand.

"Yes," he said, and rubbed her palm tenderly with his thumb. "It becomes you very nicely."

And one evening, Isabelle allowed them to pack a basket and have a picnic on the shore of Yardley Reach, the stretch of water that separated the isle from the mainland. They stepped gingerly over the rocks and laid a blanket by the water. Theodore took her hand and helped her sit.

After their supper, they stood by the water's edge. Lavinia let her gaze drift about, taking in the scene. She had never been outside Maine—indeed, never outside Dearham—but she couldn't imagine any place more beautiful. The rocks behind them were flat and craggy, and deep auburn in color. The shoreline around them was lush with trees, their pointed tops rising toward the heavens as if in worship. The water before them was calm and smooth, undulating with a light current. And above them, sweet Lord! The sky. Lavinia understood why Theodore loved it so. In the lingering sunset, it was deep blue at its highest, melting into lavender and finally to pink at the horizon. Already it dazzled with a smattering of stars, thrown about and twinkling like diamonds.

But the best part was the shore itself, which was covered not with sand but with miniature seashells—millions of them, it seemed, none larger than her fingernail. They curled and wrapped around themselves, in all colors, making the ground light up brilliantly like a rainbow. Lavinia bent at the waist and raked them with her fingers; they felt cool against her skin.

She sighed and stood, returning her attention to the water. "Such a beautiful sunset," she said. "I don't believe there's anything more beautiful on Earth."

"I believe there is."

When she turned her head, she saw that his lips were turned up into a smile, and his eyes were soft with longing. His dark hair was black in the dimmed light, and the shadows of the setting sun drew attention to the angular features of his face.

Lavinia knew what he meant, and she felt beautiful, too, standing on the rocks amidst the landscape. He held her shoulders and glided his hands over her arms and back, and she instinctively moved toward him, her back arching as she relished the sensation.

"My greatest joy is being with you," he said. "It makes me happy to share poetry with you, to look at the stars with you, to talk about all the ways we can help people in the town." Lavinia felt the tingling of tears, and blinked a few times before he continued. "Everything I do, I think of you. I wonder what you'd think of this or that. I even dream of you."

Lavinia sighed aloud. "I dream of you, too," she said, with that breathless feeling she had grown pleasantly used to.

"Sweet Lavvy," he whispered, taking her arms in his hands. "What would you say, if I were to ask if you would consider marrying me?"

"Oh," she gasped, tears springing to her eyes. "I would adore it!"

"Do you mean it?" he asked, looking at her carefully, but the excitement evident in his voice. "Would you truly like to marry me?"

"I truly would," said Lavinia, giddy with joy and barely able to contain herself. "Desperately so."

"Shall we speak with your sister and her husband? To ask for their consent?"

"Yes, we should. As soon as you'd like."

"Then it's settled," he said, smiling with triumph. "I'll call on your family tomorrow."

He brought his fingers to her head and smoothed back her hair where it had escaped its pins; then he cupped her face with his hand and brushed her cheek with his thumb. His expression turned serious.

"I was wondering," he said softly, "if I might kiss you."

Lavinia wanted very much for him to kiss her, and had imagined him kissing her many times, in as much detail as she could. Unable to speak, she nodded, then stiffened with anticipation as, his eyes drifting shut, he tilted his chin and leaned toward her. Standing straight and still, she closed her eyes and let his lips come to hers; they were soft and full, tasting of something earthy and deep. She grew dizzy, and her back turned limp as he pressed with more insistence, coaxing her open; at the sudden intrusion of his tongue, she gasped and started. His hands now splayed across her back, he paused, though the sweet, heady scent of his breath remained, and she could feel its warmth on her lips; bravely she urged them to part for him, tentatively at first, then relaxing until she took him fully in. Now immersed with him in the kiss, she sighed at the fluidity of their movements, the rush of heat that trickled into previously unknown places. His hand pressed her hip, the other hand holding her back, urging her toward him with desperation she hadn't known in him.

He broke from her and smiled breathily. "I love you, sweet Lavvy," he said. "I'm going to take care of you."

Everything about her had changed; she was to be married now, to begin her own life, and entirely new feelings had been unlocked by their kiss. "I love you, too," she said dizzily, as if from another world.

LAVINIA AND THEODORE were married in a small ceremony on the morning of the winter solstice, in Isabelle and Lyle's house just outside the village. Lavinia, wearing her best gown, a wine-colored wool dress with a pointed bodice and box-pleated skirt, carried a simple winter bouquet of fragrant yellow witch hazel and clusters of red hawthorn berries. Evergreen wreaths adorned the mantle. As she walked down the stairs, Lavinia sighed at the sight of Theodore, who wore a long gray frock coat and trousers, double-breasted waistcoat, and white cravat—and a wide smile that bespoke his excitement.

A modest lunch celebration took place afterward in Theodore and Lavinia's humble house, which was located next door to Isabelle and Lyle's house. These houses, in addition to several others on the street, were owned by none other than Mr. Mullany, the owner of the granite quarry where Lyle and Theodore worked. Lavinia and Theodore were honored when Mr. Mullany called at the house to congratulate them. They enjoyed the cheerful company of their friends and family, casting each other sly glances as the sun began to set and guests filtered out toward their houses.

When they were finally alone, Lavinia looked around her new home. It was chilly, with drafty windows and doors, and the cold night air seemed to seep up through the floorboards. But it had a nice working stove, and as the house was small, its warmth could be felt throughout. It was utilitarian but cozy, with wallpaper in whimsical patterns and simple paintings in unexpected places.

They walked upstairs, hand in hand, the steps creaking as they went. Theodore held a candle, which cast a bright halo around them, the rest of the house falling into darkness behind them.

They were utterly alone, encased in the night. Lavinia had to steady herself against the frantic beating of her heart.

They reached the entrance of their bedroom. The room was small and tidy, bare except for the essentials—a tall dresser, a writing desk, a simple wooden chair, a storage chest under the window—and a bed, with four tall posters and a simple white quilt. Lavinia paused at the entrance while Theodore stepped inside, removed his jacket, and hung it over a hook on the closet door. She had been looking forward to their wedding night and had imagined it many times, in as vivid images as possible with nothing but Isabelle's demure explanations to guide her. Now that the moment was upon her, she was eager but nervous, Isabelle's advice flying out of her memory.

She watched as Theodore pulled his suspenders down over his shoulders, her eyes wide and her hands suddenly clammy. His movements were slow and deliberate, suggesting that he too, was nervous, but trying not to let on. Facing her, he reached for the buttons of his shirt. He paused a moment, looking at her, and resumed undressing casually, though Lavinia saw the shaking of his fingers. When he stood before her, his chest bare, Lavinia's nervousness dissipated. For he was beautiful—straight, slim, and strong, his arms rippled with muscles and his torso flat and lean, his chest broad and covered with a perfect nest of dark hair. She let her eyes stray lower, bashful as she was; she had just enough time to admire the cleft of muscles leading downward from his navel, and to swallow, before he stepped toward her, and her gaze snapped upward.

Panicking, she turned to face the mirror that sat on the simple wooden dresser by the door. She looked at the pale features of her face, half illuminated by the candle, half in shadow. Theodore stood a pace behind her. Her eyes on his, she reached for the pins that held up her hair, and slowly removed them, letting her long locks cascade over her shoulders and back. She tossed her head, and the tendrils fell over her face in a beautiful mess. She was watching his reflection; he sighed as his eyes followed the tumbling of her hair.

She smiled awkwardly and reached for the back of her dress. Too bashful to ask him to help her with the clasps, she made a show of struggling, and she was relieved when he stepped behind her and began fumbling with the hook and eye closures himself. She was more at ease now that she was no longer facing him, and she relaxed enough to notice the pressure of his fingertips against her back, the way his proximity brought tingles to her skin. She heard his breath in the silence of the room, and then she felt it on her skin; he was kissing the nape of her neck as he undid the bodice, gently brushing his lips from her hairline downward toward her shoulder, and it was as if the room had suddenly grown warmer. The cool air was exhilarating against her bare skin as he slowly pulled the bodice from her shoulders and chest.

She unhooked and stepped out of her skirt and petticoat, then untied and removed her corset cover; he took the garments from her hands and draped them over the nearby chair. Her pulse beginning to race, and aware of his gaze, she reached for the strings of her corset.

"There's no end to this, is there?" Theodore asked with a chuckle as he took the strings from her fingers. She laughed, too, grateful for the joke, but she stiffened, nervous again, as he loosened the corset and added it to the pile on the chair. A hesitation, and then his hands were holding her bare shoulders. She closed her eyes at this new, intimate touch, stunned by the intensity of feeling. He drew closer, his warm palms sliding across her arms and back. She rolled her shoulders, cat-like, and released a little hum of satisfaction. He kissed her head; his breath was balmy in her hair.

She now stood in her knee-length chemise and stockings, the chilly air eliciting goosebumps on her skin. She rolled down her stockings and pulled them from her feet; feeling suddenly vulnerable and embarrassed, she scurried toward the bed, where she buried herself between the sheets.

He was watching her, his lips pulled into a straight, serious line. Silently he stepped out of his trousers and slid beside her in bed. He averted his gaze while he removed his drawers.

They lay side by side, on their backs. In the darkness of the room, Lavinia could see his silhouette in profile, and she watched the rising and falling of his chest beneath the blanket. The warmth from his body was tantalizing. She yearned to move closer to him, to embrace him and feel his skin upon her own. She wanted to know him, to learn what it felt like to be held in his arms, to understand what Isabelle had promised would be a wonderful and gratifying experience. Her entire body tingled with heaviness and warmth, and an alarming ache below; but she was shy, and frightened by her eagerness, and fearful that he would find her unladylike.

Isabelle had told her to trust her husband, that he would know what to do. So she trusted him, and waited. However, noting his panicked, wide-eyed expression, she gathered he was as unsure as she.

The bed creaked as he turned to face her. He reached for her hair as it trickled onto her pillow, and twirled the tresses between his fingers. "You look so beautiful," he said tenderly, "with your hair sprawled about."

"Thank you," she said breathlessly.

"Perhaps we should start slowly," he suggested, now tucking her hair behind her ear. Lavinia shifted onto her side. "How about if I..." He hesitated a moment, then brushed his fingers across the delicate hollow of her throat. "How about if I...if I touch you here?"

Her lips parted, and her eyes half closed. "Yes."

His fingers drifted toward her chest, then to the soft curving of her breast, which he caressed through her chemise. With great care, he pulled the chemise downward and stroked her bare breast. Her skin bristled against his touch.

"And what if," he whispered, his fingertips gliding across the pointed tip of her nipple, and playing with it gently, "I touch you here?"

She had never felt anything so good in her life. Tense, concentrated sensation surged into rivers of soft pleasure that reached through every part of her. Her chest rose and fell against his fingers. She wanted to cry out, but swallowed instead. "Yes," she breathed, daring to touch his foot with her own.

His fingertip trailed along the graceful curve of her waist and down her hip, alighting the nerves in its wake. His fingers pressed against her thigh, slipping under the chemise and cupping her backside.

"And here?" he said shakily.

Her legs twisted as she struggled to bear the aching pressure at her center. She said nothing, but leaned closer, her cheek rubbing his.

His heavy breath upon her lips, he kissed her, tugging her lips with his own, his hand sliding further under her chemise and between her thighs. He moved his thumb, nudging just inside her.

"And here?"

"Yes," she gasped. "Please, yes."

He said nothing more, but explored her with his thumb, tentatively parting her with his fingers. Lavinia now cared not for modesty, and she moaned aloud. She edged her hips closer, and halted with shock.

Isabelle had confided in her about male anatomy. Somehow Lavinia had not taken her seriously. The drama of it had seemed impossible, almost laughable. Tonight, however, lying in bed with a panting Theodore, Lavinia saw with certainty that there was nothing joking about what Isabelle had told her. Her mind rushing, she took a moment to reconcile the gentleness of her husband with the brash, aggressive thing that had happened to his body. She was frightened but curious, and compelled by an instinct too primitive to understand. She felt the heat from his body, could sense the intensity of his expression as he looked at her through the darkness. She lifted her gaze to meet his, then downward toward where their bodies connected.

Cautiously she raised her hand to his naked chest. He was so muscular here, so strong. She slid her hand over his lean torso, marveling at the layer of dark hair, until it disappeared beneath the blanket. His breathing deepened, and she felt his feet fidgeting below. She took a breath and lowered her hand.

She let her thumb and fingers surround him, her fingertips toying along the edge. Feeling increasingly brave, she lowered her hand farther until her palm and fingers wrapped around the hard shaft. She squeezed gently, and he groaned. Beneath her fingers, he stiffened and pulsed.

Her eyes darted to his face. His eyes were closed and his lips parted. She was amazed she had this power over him, to make him twist and gasp. She gripped him tighter and moved her hand. His hips swayed toward her, and he groaned again.

"Lavvy," he whispered, brushing his lips against her cheek. He reached for her waist and pulled her closer. "Maybe let's not start slowly. Maybe let's—"

She interrupted him with a kiss. Still gripping him, she slid her other hand around his shoulder and wrapped it around the back of his head. After a few heated moments, breathless with anticipation and emboldened by his ragged sighs, she pulled her lips from his. "Maybe let's not talk anymore," she whispered.

His eyes drifted shut, and he let her kiss envelop him. She shifted onto her back, and he followed her, still locked with her in a kiss, until he was leaning over her. He brought his hand upward and cupped her face, his fingers burying into her hair. She lifted her knee, and he slid between her legs. Her chemise was around her waist; together they pulled it over her chest and shoulders, then tossed it to the floor. Lavinia glided her hands across his powerful form, relishing his masculinity. His full weight was now on top of her, his hair-covered chest pressed against the fullness of her breasts, the hardness of him unmistakable evidence of his need for her. She felt desired, and womanly, and it all conspired to seduce her further. She closed her eyes, waiting for him to take her, and steeling herself; Isabelle had warned her there may be pain, and now that Lavinia had acquainted herself with the full length of him, she worried that she couldn't possibly accommodate him.

His hand was fumbling under the blanket as he struggled to position himself. She found herself lifting her hips in encouragement, her fear eclipsed by instinct and primal need. She watched his face as he concentrated. Oh, but he was handsome. She pressed her hands against the taut muscles of his shoulders and back, and her heart pattered. She saw the uncertainty and apprehension in his face, and she swooned inside.

Finally, and quite suddenly, he found her, nudging just at the entrance of her. Lavinia inhaled sharply, her eyes wide. She braced herself, her nervous body closing against him.

Theodore, however, now seemed confident and eager. He grazed her face with the backs of his fingers, and his eyes locked with hers. "Oh Lavvy," he said, his voice hoarse. "Lavvy, I love you."

Her blood tingled, and she felt her muscles loosen. He pressed his cheek to hers, and began pushing into her, his fingers squeezing her shoulders and his skin flushed with sweat.

She burned where he entered her. She cried out, feeling stretched and pulled apart. He stopped and kissed her cheek, his body shaking.

"Are you...Are you all right?"

She looked away, her face contorted with discomfort. She nodded.

"Does it...Am I..."

"No," she whispered. She swallowed. "A little."

He said nothing, but waited patiently, his entire body quivering and tense.

She took a deep breath and wriggled, adjusting herself around him. Having composed herself, she moved her hips upward, inviting him to continue. The movement made her grimace, but something pleasant shivered in her deepest core.

He drove further until he had filled her completely. Her body simultaneously fought against this invasion and closed around him. He seemed to have forgotten his suggestion to go slowly; he writhed smoothly inside her, having crossed from innocence to understanding.

"Dear God," he cried, with evident disbelief. He was thrusting mercilessly, his hands gripping her. "Dear God, Lavvy," he laughed. "Oh, good God..."

She was sore, and confused, and she was desperately trying to process everything that was happening to her. But she was captivated by his heavy breathing, his enthusiasm, the way his fingers stroked through her hair. She had adjusted to the fullness that had stretched her tight, cautiously enjoying now a different kind of fire. She relaxed her thighs further, letting him lead her. She concentrated on the molten feeling that gathered gradually in the innermost parts of her.

He was no longer laughing, but had rather turned serious, his deep groans seeming to erupt from him involuntarily. She was surprised by the powerful effect these sounds had on her; they seemed to drive her own passion, igniting sparks in her belly that shot all the way to her fingers and toes. She allowed herself a sigh and closed her eyes. Every movement brought more sensation, and she invited it, closing her thighs around him and undulating her hips with his. She clutched his back with her fingers as his lips wet her throat, then gripped the back of his head, mussing his hair in desperate, messy clumps. He kissed the sensitive skin behind her ear, and she lifted her chin toward the ceiling, heart thumping.

"And now? Is this all right?" he asked her, now kissing her cheek. He grunted as she ran her hands over his hips and gripped him from behind.

"Oh," she cried by way of answer, moving seamlessly with him. His scent deepened as sweat gathered at his hairline, and she inhaled greedily. She said nothing more, but wondered at the tightening tenderness, a feeling of rising that made little sense as she lay beneath him. Her eyes flew open.

"Theodore," she stammered.

"Yes, Lavvy," he replied breathily into her ear.

She couldn't find her voice; her eyes drifted shut. She had begun to feel frightened, and she wanted to tell him to stop, even as her body begged to sink into the first fluttering vibrations. He was pushing harder, more insistently, oblivious to her panic—and all the while, with every motion, she was lifted higher, the tension tight and tingling, threatening to burst. She felt herself approaching a precipice, and fought to push it away; but the promise of relief was too strong. A moment of suspension, and she fell from the edge; she coasted through waves of unimaginable bliss, through her own cries registering the sound of her name as he sighed it into her ear. His body braced suddenly against hers, and his movements elongated until finally he relaxed. Her hips instinctively slowing, she lay back in wonder; even as she relished the fading delight of the final spasms, she was dumbstruck. She had had no idea her body was capable of this, that two people could create this together. Vaguely she considered how little she knew, and how much was possible. She barely knew what to make of it.

Having recollected her wits, she realized they were drenched with sweat. She pulled the blanket down his back to his hips. The cold winter air on her hot skin refreshed and calmed her. She sank back and smiled, paralyzed, overcome by a delicious sense of peace.

He slid onto his back and lay beside her, still panting.

"Mercy," he breathed, eyes closed.

Lavinia nodded in agreement, staring up at the ceiling, amazed.

He turned his head to look at her. "What was it like for you?" he asked. "Was it..."

She took a deep breath as her heartbeat finally began to slow. "Yes," she said, unable to suppress a sly grin. "Yes, it was."

They lay in silence for a few moments.

"We can go to church now, if you'd like," Lavinia said.

Theodore's brow furrowed. He turned to her again. "What do you mean?"

"I assumed that's what you wanted, judging by the number of times you called for God."

Theodore stared at her, his eyes wide. Gradually humor crept into his face until his eyes sparkled and his lips curved into a wide grin.

He bellowed with laughter and pulled her close. Lavinia smiled contentedly as he rubbed her back and squeezed her hips, giddy from the excitement of their wedding night and delighted by the enhanced intimacy it had ushered in. "Yes," he said, gasping for breath as his laughter subsided. "Yes, you are right, my sweet Lavvy. And the only church in which I wish to worship is lying naked in my bed."

CHAPTER 3

"*I remember those days,*" *said Nick, with a wistful smile. "Just starting out, just getting to know each other. Then building on that as time goes by.*"

"*Young love,*" *said the man in brown. "There's nothing like it.*"

"*I don't know,*" *said Nick. "I don't think age matters. I wasn't so young when I got married.*"

"*How old were you?*"

"*Thirty-six.*"

"*Still young,*" *said the man in brown, tossing his hand in the air.*

"*It's nice that she enjoyed Maine with him,*" *said Nick. "Just like I do with my wife. I guess some things never change.*"

"*Oh, that kind of thing never changes, of course. But some things do.*"

"*Something changed for Lavinia and Theodore?*"

"*It was nothing more than a chance encounter. But sometimes, that's all it takes.*"

THEODORE AND LAVINIA were blissfully happy together. They didn't have a lot of money, but they didn't need it. They had the beautiful Maine landscape around them. They had their cozy little house near Yardley Reach, and the simple comforts of home. In each other, they had true, deep affection and friendship. They had a warm bed and loving arms to come home to. And it was enough.

During the day, they worked hard. Lavinia sewed and mended for the villagers, and she loved her work, though her fingers were red and sore. Theodore worked at the quarry, drilling holes and assisting as the huge stone slabs were hoisted onto the schooners that would carry them to faraway ports. He came home each night tired and dirty, and eager for the quiet of their home. Lavinia rubbed his feet, pleased by the euphoric smile on his face as she soothed his aches and pains. She helped scrub the dirt from his face, neck, and fingers, though she found attractive the rough, masculine look of him when he was gritty with his work.

Young, newly wed, and very much in love, they looked forward to retiring together at night, when they forgot the stresses of making a living and the scarcity of food on the table, and reveled in the comfort of darkness, which eclipsed everything but the warmth of the bed and the joy of being entangled in each other. Lavinia was surprised and delighted by Theodore's passion and eagerness.

Lavinia loved Theodore and yearned to have children with him. She adored her little niece, Betsy, and wanted to experience motherhood for herself. She watched Isabelle comforting and playing with her daughter, and was struck with pangs of longing. But months passed, and still Lavinia was not with child. She prayed she'd be granted her wish. In the meantime, she was thankful for her kind, loving husband and the life he had given her.

One day, Theodore came home from work even more excited than usual. Lavinia was in the parlor, sewing a dress for an affluent woman from town. It was a clear, warm evening in late spring, nearly summer. Lavinia sat by the open window, working quickly in the final blue light of dusk.

She looked up as he approached with swift, long strides and knelt before her, taking her hands in his.

"Sweet Lavvy," he said, kissing her hand, carefully avoiding the needle she held tightly between her fingers; he hadn't even given her time to lay down her work. "I have news for you, news of the best kind."

Lavinia stared at him, wide-eyed, as he looked up at her, his face bright. Surprised, she waited for him to elaborate.

"How would you," he said slowly, his voice tight with latent energy, "like a brand new sewing machine?"

Her eyebrows furrowed. "Yes..." she began with caution. "That would be lovely..."

"What if I told you, my dear, that you will have your sewing machine, and so much more?"

Lavinia didn't know what to say. She felt he was leading up to something, but she didn't know what, and therefore didn't know if she was in favor of it.

His eyes widened at her silence. "Well, sweet Lavvy?" he prodded, a smile curving his lips. "Wouldn't you like it? It would make your work so much quicker and easier. Best of all, it would be kinder on your pretty little fingers." He kissed her fingertips, one by one, sweetly, as if they were children.

Lavinia laughed, delighted, her skin prickling pleasantly at the tender touch of his lips. "Theodore, dear, what is this about?"

Theodore replaced her hand in her lap and stepped backward until he reached an old armchair, its once bright blue fabric faded into a pale gray. He sat with his hands folded on his knees as he leaned forward, watching her intently.

"Lavvy," he said. "Something happened today, something unusual. I met a man, purely by chance. It could only be destiny. It could only be ordained by the stars."

"What?" she said impatiently, bopping up and down in her chair. "Good heavens, what is it? You must tell me!"

"Well then, I will begin my story," he said, his voice once again picking up speed. "You see, a man came to the quarry today. He is the brother of Mr. Mullany."

"Mr. Mullany is the owner of the quarry," said Lavinia.

"Precisely, and his brother is the owner of the ship that brings the granite to the West Indies. Mr. Mullany's brother was walking along the quarry's edge with Mr. Mullany while I was taking my lunch by the shaded patch of grass under the trees. I was looking around, admiring the clarity of the day, when I noticed a commotion out of the corner of my eye. Straight ahead, a chipmunk scurried in front of the oxen that were pulling the carts. The carts had just been emptied, you see, and were carrying no rock. They were being readied to receive more blocks of granite, to be brought to the railroad. Anyway, the chipmunk spooked the oxen, which reared backward and bolted!" To demonstrate, Theodore struck his hand outward in an abrupt, sudden motion, his eyes wide with amazement.

"Oh, dear," said Lavinia. "That must have been frightening."

"Indeed, it was, especially since Mr. Mullany's brother stood only ten yards away, oblivious to the whole occurrence!"

"Good Lord," Lavinia said, more urgently now. "What happened next? Was the poor man trampled?"

"Ah, and now we come to the most exciting part! He was not trampled, sweet Lavvy, no. As I said, I was watching from the patch of grass under the trees. I stood upright"—here, he stood upright—"and called out to him, 'Mr. Mullany!' but I could see there was no time. I dropped my lunch and ran, as fast as I could, to Mr. Mullany's brother, and pushed him from the oxen's path just in the nick of time."

"Oh, darling!"

"And," said Theodore, calming now, and sitting once again, "the good man was saved."

Lavinia dropped her work and sprang from her chair, now bending over her husband as he sat, and wrapping her arms around his back and chest. She kissed him endlessly on the head, then took his face in her hands and kissed his lips. "My hero," she breathed, sitting on his lap. "You saved his life. What a brave, strong man I married."

"No, my dear, I did what any man would do."

"Well, what did he say? Was Mr. Mullany's brother hurt at all?"

"No, he had not even a scratch, though he was dusty as the devil, and white as a ghost from the shock. By now many men had come upon us, including Mr. Mullany. Both he and his brother shook my hand and thanked me. I daresay Mr. Mullany's brother was close to tears."

"I can't say I blame him," said Lavinia, close to tears herself. "What a dreadfully close encounter."

"Indeed, it was. But, by the grace of God, no one was hurt. Quite the contrary. The incident has improved our condition a hundredfold. You see, Mr. Mullany's brother offered to reward me for what I had done. I told him I could not accept any money. A man's life is priceless."

"I agree, wholeheartedly," said Lavinia, swelling with warmth and pride in her husband. "I'm glad you responded as you did."

"Thank you, Lavvy. I am, too. But Mr. Mullany's brother is a wealthy, benevolent man, and he insisted on repaying me, somehow. When I refused payment, he asked if there was something my wife might like. Well, I've no need of a reward myself, but I don't have the heart to refuse something for my wife, now, do I?" He smiled. "I told him that my wife's little fingers were sore from sewing, and that she was such a hard-working, dutiful wife, and that as a matter of fact, I wouldn't mind her having a sewing machine. Mr. Mullany's brother laughed and clapped me on the back, and he promised he'd send one on the morrow."

Lavinia laughed, too. "How generous of him. And how wonderful of you, dear." She leaned forward and met him in a flurry of kisses.

"But that's not all," he said, turning serious. "Mr. Mullany's brother insisted on a gesture of gratitude. I said I do have a dream, a longing that rests deep in my heart. And that's when I told him."

"Told him what?"

"I told him I had always wanted to go to sea."

Lavinia now understood. Her smile faded.

Theodore continued, "Mr. Mullany's brother told me he would find a spot for me on his ship's next voyage. I'm going to sea, Lavinia. I'm going to sea."

Lavinia stared at him blankly. She was unsure what to say, and therefore said nothing.

"But, that's not even the best part," Theodore said, looking up at her, a smile creeping slowly into his eyes. "Mr. Mullany's brother is an old bachelor. He had named his boat the *Angelina*, after the woman he loved, who would not have him. He said it was time for him to accept that he would not win her heart, and to rename his boat. He asked me to tell him about my wife, and I told him I had the prettiest, most charming wife in the world. And he said it would be his honor if I would allow him to rename his boat after my wife."

Lavinia felt quite overwhelmed. She raised her eyebrows. "You joke with me."

"No, I'm quite serious. I sail to the West Indies, one week from today—on Mr. Mullany's ship, the *Sweet Lavvy*."

She frowned and slid from his lap, then sat gingerly in her chair once more. She didn't know what she had expected him to tell her when he said he had news, but it certainly wasn't this. She supposed he wanted her to be excited for him, that he hoped she would encourage him to fulfill this lifelong dream. But all she could feel was dread.

"You're skeptical," he said gently, rising from his chair and then kneeling before her. He took her hands in his, and squeezed. "And rightly so. But Lavvy, just think. I earn only ninety-five cents a day at the quarry. A crewman's pay is scant. But maybe one day, if I become a captain, I could bring home more than twice that. And if we have a baby one day, a little girl as pretty as you," he added, his lips turned up in a little smile, his wide blue eyes locked with hers, "she would have everything she wanted."

Lavinia softened. She so wanted a child with him. Hearing him express his longing, too, and his longing to provide for his child, made her feel warm with love and anticipation. She melted further as he kissed her delicately on the lips, then kissed her again, more intimately, his hands rubbing up and down her thighs.

He pulled away, and her eyes turned sorrowful.

"But I'll miss you," she said.

"That is my one reservation, of course," he said, kissing her hand and watching her with solemn eyes. "The thought of not seeing you every day is dreadful." He took a stray tendril of her hair between his fingers and played with it for a moment, then tenderly tucked it behind her ear. "I love you so much, more than anything in the world. We were created for each other, Lavvy. Ever since we met in the cemetery on the solstice, I've just known it. Our spirits called to each other that day, and have been inter-mingled ever since. If anything or anyone could keep me from leaving, it's you."

She sighed at the poetry of his statement, and squeezed his hand as it rested in hers.

"But..." he went on, now looking to the side, and frowning. "I feel in my bones that I must do this. I need to feel the vastness of the sea. I need to see the stars as they're reflected in the waves and to discover what's beyond the horizon. Being out on the water, with no land around me, just the Earth and me..." He looked at her, his eyes beseeching. "I struggle to explain myself. But I was meant to see the stars. My spirit yearns to fly." He shrugged. "I must do it," he said simply, his frown deepening.

Her eyes filled with tears, but she firmed her face and held them back. She would not be weak and pitiful, nor would she trample on his dream. She knew he spoke the truth. She knew he would not leave her unless he had to. And she knew she could not lay her head upon her pillow having denied him this.

"I understand," she made herself say, albeit shakily. "It's just... It's just so dangerous."

"Sweet Lavvy," he said. His voice was low and serious, and he watched her earnestly. "I will come back to you. Make no mistake. I will return."

Lavinia didn't know whether she believed him, but she nodded and fell to him as he embraced her. His absence would be awful; she felt she couldn't bear it. But she wanted him to explore, as he had always yearned to do. She was glad he would find something his soul had been missing. And she was eager for him to return, a more complete Theodore, and to share with her all he had learned.

ONE WEEK LATER, Theodore left for sea. Standing on the dock on that fine summer morning, the heady air in her lungs and the salty breeze tumbling in her skirts, the seagulls playing over the water, Lavinia watched the scene solemnly. The sailors readied the ship, calling orders and hopping about, preparing to begin a new journey—and despite her sadness, the energy was contagious. Though she herself was content in their little town, and though the thought of being tossed about by the waves made her stomach lurch, she was excited for Theodore.

Theodore was bringing to sea with him three very special items. He had a pocket watch, given to him by his father on the day he married Lavinia. He had a tiny wooden case, in which he carried a lock of Lavinia's hair. And finally, though they had bought his slops from the purser, Lavinia had worked tirelessly to make his jacket herself.

As she stood with her sailor upon his first voyage, she swelled with pride at the image of him in his uniform. He had spent many hours in the last week under the tutelage of the ship's captain, and he was eager to test his skills. He looked at ease and natural among the other sailors, so strong and handsome. Lavinia sighed as she watched him. He had told her sailing was his destiny, that he was meant for great voyages, and she had to agree. She would miss him desperately, though.

Finally it was time to part. Theodore embraced her, his eyes closed and his nose and lips buried in her hair, and she held him tight, deliberately absorbing the feel of his chest pressed to hers and the musky, masculine scent of his hair and skin.

"Before you leave...I have something for you," she told him, reaching into the pocket of her dress and withdrawing a small velvet bag. She held it for him, and he took it.

He tipped the bag so the item inside fell gently into the palm of his hand. It was a gold watch fob, small and simple, with a delicate engraving. Theodore's expression was serious as he read. "'TS + LL, winter solstice '56.'" He looked at her and smiled soberly, though his eyes sparkled. "The happiest day of my life."

She swallowed, holding back emotion. "It's also a locket," she said, bringing her hand to his and turning the fob over a couple of times with her fingers. She gingerly opened it. "It's for your watch and—"

"And your hair." As he finished her sentence, he pulled the tiny case from the pocket of his jacket and moved the lock of hair into the locket. He pressed it shut, then attached the fob to his watch chain. "My darling," he whispered, pulling her once again into a tight embrace. "Thank you for this. I'll keep it close to my heart every moment."

"I love you," she murmured into his ear, her entire body tingling as his hands roamed over her shoulders, back, and waist, taking her in for the last time.

"I love you, too," he whispered, kissing the side of her face and the small places of her neck, making her swoon. "You cannot imagine the intensity of my love for you."

"I can imagine it," she said, bringing her lips to his.

They kissed for many moments, her fingers in his hair, his hands on her back holding her close.

"My dear, did you see?" He pulled away and gestured toward the ship with a nod of his chin, then turned back to her. "*Sweet Lavvy.*"

Lavinia smiled ruefully. The words "Sweet Lavvy" shone in freshly painted red letters on the side of the ship. She had noticed it first thing.

"It's lovely," she said. "I'll always be with you."

"And I with you." A kind smile touched his lips. "You'll think of me whenever you use your new sewing machine."

"Oh, I don't think I can use that sewing machine. Not until you come home. It will make me miss you even more."

"I wish you would. You're even more lovely when you're bending over your work, your eyes so concentrated, your pretty fingers so lithe and quick." With a boyish smile, he brought her hand to his lips and kissed her fingertips, making her blush and sigh. "It makes me happy to see you use it."

"And you will see me use it again, when you come home."

"Already I can't wait." His expression turned thoughtful. "You know what today is, don't you?"

Lavinia shook her head.

His lips turned upward in one corner, a sly little grin making him look devilishly handsome. "It's the summer solstice."

Lavinia's eyes softened, and she smiled.

"You know what that means," he went on, rubbing her shoulders with his hands. "It's a good time for journeys. The spirits are about. The air is full of energy to help our spirits find each other."

Lavinia sighed and embraced him, once again wooed by his belief in the beauty and connection of the universe. She found consolation in the thought, in spite of her skepticism.

They turned their heads toward the ship as the commotion

increased: the ship was ready to leave, and it was time for him to go.

He took her face in his hands, peered into her eyes, and spoke softly. "I will return to you. I promise. When I took you as my wife, I vowed this to you."

She sighed inwardly, drawn to the warmth of his eyes and the kindness in his expression. Tears pricked at the corners of her eyes, and she let them come.

"I love you," she told him again. "I will wait for you."

They embraced once more, and she let him go. She stood on the dock for a long time, until the ship was far off in the distance, a mere speck on the horizon that parted the sky and the sea.

CHAPTER 4

"*So that's how Theodore left his young wife and began his journey," said the man in brown.*

Nick had been listening intently. "It must have been hard for them to say goodbye."

"No doubt about it. Can you imagine saying goodbye to your wife like that?"

A dull ache enveloped Nick's heart. He shook his head. "No. I can't."

"Back in those days," said the man in brown, "you couldn't just pick up a phone and call a person, of course. Theodore, at least, was occupied with his life at sea, taking care of the ship and enjoying the glorious new sights. Poor Lavinia had nothing to do but go back to her sewing, pining for him and hoping he was safe."

"Did they write letters?"

"The sailors could exchange incoming and outgoing mail at port. But they didn't dock at port often, and letters took weeks or months arrive. And anyway, Theodore only had the chance to write one letter before..." His voice trailed off.

"Before what?" asked Nick, with an encroaching feeling of dread. "He didn't die at sea, of course," he added hopefully.

"Well, now," said the man in brown, gesturing with his index finger. "That's where the story gets interesting."

THE VOYAGE to the West Indies was to last two months. Lavinia went about her life as usual. She worked busily by hand during the day while her sewing machine sat tucked unused in the corner of the parlor, seeming to wait patiently for Theodore's return. She spent as much time as she could with her sister and niece in the evenings, and she climbed into bed alone each night, yearning for Theodore. The weather was warm now, and she slept with the windows open and the curtains parted, gazing at the star-filled sky and imagining Theodore looking at the very same stars. A warm breeze fluttered the curtains and blew in the scents of the Maine summer. Lavinia thought she could even smell his thick, musky fragrance if she concentrated hard enough. She thought of him on the undulating waves of the ocean, and wished she could hold him against her.

Two months passed, and the *Sweet Lavvy* did not return. This was not cause to worry, as voyages often took longer than expected, depending on the weather and the conditions of the wind and sea. But when three months passed, then four, then five —with no letters from port—rumor began to circulate that the *Sweet Lavvy* had been lost.

Isabelle wept one chilly late autumn afternoon as she and Lavinia strolled along the docks, gazing out toward the sea. Already the water would be brutally cold; the harsh Maine winter loomed just ahead, making the *Sweet Lavvy*'s return seem that much more unlikely.

"My sweet sister, something has surely happened," Isabelle cried, dabbing at her eyes with a handkerchief. "I'm so sorry. I just don't see how poor Theodore can come home."

"He said he would come back to me," said Lavinia, feeling oddly calm. "He promised."

And she remained calm even when, on the day of their wedding anniversary, she received word that the ship's stern had washed ashore in Boston, the red letters verifying beyond a doubt that the *Sweet Lavvy* was gone.

Isabelle and her family visited her at home that winter's night so Isabelle could relay the news. Her husband Lyle sat in a straight-backed chair while little Betsy played quietly with a doll on the floor. Lavinia sat beside her sister on the settee in the chilly little parlor. A single oil lamp cast a warm, flickering glow along the walls and ceiling. Lavinia, in a white cotton dress with flower-shaped buttons and a high lace collar, stared straight ahead into the darkness, blank-faced, unheeding of her sister's tears. Outside the halo cast by the lantern, the light faded gradually into black, giving the impression of infinite nothingness.

Isabelle sniffled and regarded her sister with worried eyes. "You've barely said a word," she said, placing her cold hand on her sister's. "You must be devastated. And on your wedding anniversary, too. Poor dear. I think it would do you good to talk about it."

Lavinia knew her sister was right. But she felt nothing. She simply couldn't believe Theodore was gone.

"Darling," her sister said softly. "What are you thinking?"

Lavinia looked at her. "I was thinking," she said, "that today is the winter solstice."

Isabelle furrowed her brow. "What in heaven's name does that have to do with anything?"

Lavinia turned her head back toward the darkness. Her eyes caught sight of the long-neglected sewing machine in the corner. She felt a momentary catch in her throat.

Isabelle began shaking with tears once more. "Come, darling. You're in shock. You will stay with us tonight."

"Yes, of course," agreed Lyle kindly. "We insist."

Betsy began singing a soft, happy tune, rocking her doll in her arms. Lavinia watched her for a long moment, then shook her head.

"No. I want to stay in my house, in my bed."

"You're not in your right mind. You could be a danger to yourself. I can't allow it."

Lavinia stood and embraced her sister, then pulled away, smiling sweetly.

"I'm not a danger. I promise. You go on home," she said, "and leave me be."

And with that, she walked evenly up the stairs, in the dark, leaving her baffled family in wonder.

DEARHAM WAS A SMALL TOWN, and news of the loss of the *Sweet Lavvy* spread quickly. Many of the sailors were from neighboring communities and were unknown to the residents of Dearham, but several of the men had been born and bred there, and were mourned by everyone in town. The townspeople immediately flocked to the families of those lost, offering love, support, and sympathy.

A group of young women called on Lavinia the next morning, bearing baskets of apples, pastries, and other items to comfort her. They stood solemnly outside her door in their capes and bonnets, shivering in the cold and stamping their booted feet as they waited for her to answer.

"I would not be surprised if you receive no answer," called Isabelle from next door, emerging bundled up in her cloak and gloves, shutting the door behind her. She crossed the yard toward the women, her breath drifting up like smoke in the frigid air. When she stood beside them, she placed her hand on the back of the woman standing closest to her, her face gentle with gratitude. "She was not well when I left her last night."

"What a terrible tragedy," lamented one of the women. "They had only just married."

"Poor thing," said another. "It must be such a terrible shock."

Their solemn chatter was interrupted by the opening of the front door. All faces turned toward Lavinia, who stood in the doorway in a pale blue day dress with a pretty lace collar, her silky raven locks hanging freely down her slender neck and over her back to her waist. Her face was rosy and bright, her eyes glowing. She smiled at them from inside the house.

"Lavinia," said Isabelle, cautiously. "Are you all right, dear?"

"We've brought you some things," said one of the women. "We all feel awful about what's happened."

"Yes," said another, as the women murmured agreement. "We want to help you through this. May we come in and make you some tea?"

Lavinia's smile turned quizzical. "Help me?"

"Y-yes," said the first woman, looking around at her companions with confusion.

"But why ever would I need help?"

All the women stared at her, dumbfounded.

Isabelle stepped forward and took her sister's hands.

"Darling," she said. "You've lost your husband." She paused, her eyes locked into her sister's. "Do you feel nothing?"

Lavinia took in the worried faces of her friends. "Oh," she said, shaking her head a little. "Of course. Yes, it's a shame, about Theodore." She indicated the basket they had brought. "Is this for me?"

She reached for it. The woman held it out to her, speechless.

"Thank you so very much," said Lavinia as her hand gripped the basket, her voice cheerful. "You are all so kind. I truly am fortunate to have such thoughtful friends."

She made to close the door. Isabelle stopped her.

"Don't you want some company, dear?"

Lavinia smiled politely. "No," she said, with a little shrug. "I don't believe I do."

She bit her lower lip, glanced at the party with an inscrutable expression, and closed the door.

The women stood in silence for many moments.

"Well," said one finally. "The nerve."

"Indeed," said another. "And the shame. Why, she was wearing blue! Not even one day since she learned of poor Mr. Sewall's passing, and she's not even in mourning!"

"Ladies, ladies," said a third, slowing them by gesturing with her hands. "Clearly, Lavinia is in shock to act so outrageously. The poor thing is out of her senses."

"Thank you," said Isabelle sharply, glaring at the women with anger in her eyes. "At least one of my friends has compassion. It's plain to see my sister is not in her right mind. She is beside herself with grief. Maybe you can dismiss her in her time of need, but I cannot." She clutched the doorknob and tried to open the door, but it was locked. She banged on the door, begging Lavinia to let her inside.

"Lavinia! Please, darling. Let your sister in."

There was no reply. The women began dispersing, muttering to each other under their breaths. Isabelle felt tears spring to her eyes.

"Lavvy," she cried. "Please. I'm worried about you."

She stood straighter as she heard the sound of the door being unlocked. Lavinia opened the door a crack and peered through.

Isabelle frowned. "You must let me in, Lavvy. It's not healthy to hold this inside. Lean on me, cry with me. Just do...something!"

Lavinia opened the door farther. As she did so, Isabelle glanced into the house. Her eyes widened.

She looked at her sister, her expression blank. "Your sewing machine. You've brought it out again."

"Yes, I have. It was time."

"I find the timing rather odd."

Lavinia studied her sister, then reached out and placed her hand gently on her shoulder. She looked into her eyes and smiled.

"I love you, Isabelle," she said. "No words can adequately convey how much I appreciate your tending to me." She paused a moment, furrowing her brow with thought. "I can't explain it. But something has happened."

"Of course something has happened! Your husband is dead."

Lavinia shook her head. "No, that's not what I meant. Just please. Leave me be, for now. Come back later, or tomorrow." She regarded her sister with a peculiar expression, then withdrew her hand, smiled awkwardly, and shut the door. Isabelle stared after her in the cold, bewildered and heartbroken.

CHAPTER 5

*T*he man in brown sighed. "As you can imagine, before sunset that day, the whole town knew about Lavinia's strange behavior. Some saw it as shameful and disrespectful. But most people assumed that Lavinia had gone mad, that she was unable to handle her grief over Theodore's death and that a breakdown would happen at any time."

"Did it?"

The man shook his head. "No. In fact, as the weeks passed, Lavinia was cheerful as ever. She acted as if nothing had happened. She continued taking work from the ladies of the town, who pitied and indulged her as if she were a child playing make believe—and by using her sewing machine, she was able to take on more work than ever before. She carried out her errands in town as usual, chatting with the grocer and the butcher as she always had. People were kind to her. They rarely talked to her about Theodore. On the occasion that they did, Lavinia's face grew serious, and she appeared to breathe more heavily. She nodded at their expressions of sympathy, but she never discussed his death or gave any indication that she was sad. She merely stared with a faraway look in her eyes. This strange reaction upset and even frightened people. So they ceased mentioning Theodore and let it be the elephant in the room."

"What about Isabelle? Did she try to make her sister talk?"

"Isabelle was wary of pushing her sister, whom she believed to be in a delicate state, especially given the close quarters. You see, Lavinia consented to moving in with Isabelle and her family. Isabelle couldn't help but notice that something wasn't right. And Lavinia had always been such a level-headed girl. It was hard for Isabelle to believe she could deceive herself, or anyone else."

"It's too bad Lavinia had to move," said Nick. "She probably didn't want to leave the house she had shared with Theodore."

"Ah, yes, well...I gather she felt Theodore remained in her heart. Besides, as happy and independent as Lavinia was, even she couldn't deny that without Theodore's income, it would be hard for her to make the rent on her own. And she helped Isabelle as much as she could. But the situation lent itself to more questions. Now that she and Lavinia were living together, Isabelle started noticing strange things happening, things for which there were no explanations. She didn't know what was going on, but she couldn't help feeling it was all connected."

Nick was silent a moment. His brows furrowed thoughtfully. "So why wasn't Lavinia sad? Was she unable to handle Theodore's death?"

"That's just the problem." The man in brown leaned forward, excitement latent in his voice. "People began speculating that Lavinia believed Theodore had come home after all. She became the talk of the town. At first, people laughed a little at her expense. But, soon what they saw as her undying love for her husband became endearing. They saw her eccentricity as part of her charm, and they accepted it."

"Hmm," said Nick, folding his arms across his chest. His thoughts drifted to his wife, to her sweet smile and cheerful laugh, to the way he looked forward to coming home to her every day and the way she let him know she was happy to see him, too. He thought of their shared history, how they had fallen in love quickly and built on their undeniable connection ever since, how they were raising children together and how their love grew deeper with time. "That wouldn't surprise me," he said. "I can understand her refusal to accept his death."

"Ah," said the man in brown, with a mischievous grin. "But what makes you think she was wrong?"

"*Then the ship didn't sink?*"

"*No, the ship sank.*"

"*Then Theodore managed to survive.*"

"*I didn't say that, either.*"

Nick regarded him blankly. "*I don't understand.*"

"*Neither did Isabelle. But she was determined to get to the bottom of it.*"

WINTER WAS RELENTLESS, but beautiful. Snowfall turned the bare, prickly fields of late autumn into shimmering seas of white —pristine except for the zigzagging paw prints of Maine's heartiest creatures. Tree branches were encrusted with ice, and as one plodded through town or through the forest, one heard them crackling and tinkling. The snow-topped mountains in the distance seemed to blend in with the clouds. And Yardley Reach froze over, to the delight of the children, who took to the ice in their skates. Many a merchant dragged his horse and sleigh across the Reach, conducting business as usual. But then tugboats were brought to break up the ice and clear the way, and life returned to normal.

Soon the crisp smell of winter dissipated, and the air became sweet with the promise of spring. The sky turned from white to blue as the sun appeared a little earlier each day. The ice melted from the treetops, dripping to the ground in a constant stream and pockmarking with holes the snowdrifts beneath. One's boots were always wet, and one needed to stomp the heavy brown slush from the soles before walking indoors. Activity increased in town and on the docks, and a few brave sparrows pecked about for the earliest signs of food.

One day, Isabelle decided to go for a walk. But rather than a leisurely stroll down the road or a cleansing hike through the woods, she left Betsy with Lavinia and began the vigorous trek to the granite quarry to see her husband. In her hand she carried a little basket, which contained a couple of scones Lavinia had baked that morning, and also a small jar of clotted cream.

It was a cheerful, sunny day, and the workers were taking their lunch outside. They sat atop a staircase of enormous slabs of granite, their legs dangling from the sides—large, strong men looking miniscule against the smooth stone beneath them and the grandeur of the mountains on the horizon. The long arms of the derricks jutted forward over the precipice of the quarry like giraffes preparing to drink from the river. In the quarry, the earth was split apart, its walls formed into strange uneven squares. On the edge stood the stone shed, a boxy building sided with dark wood planks. Isabelle slowed her stride as she approached. She picked her husband out in an instant, and she smiled. He was a tall, lanky fellow, with a high forehead and auburn mutton chops. He stood with his arms folded over his camel-colored vest and gray-checked shirt, his back relaxed, as he laughed at a joke one of the workers had just told. Isabelle loved seeing her husband with his men; he was amiable and kind, and she knew the men respected him for it.

He turned in her direction, and his face brightened further. Excusing himself, he approached her with long strides, placed his hands on her shoulders, and kissed her forehead.

"Well, this is a pleasant surprise, my love!" He smiled boyishly as she lifted the lid of the basket, revealing the treats inside. "What have I done to deserve all this?"

"Nothing, and everything," she said. "This is just to thank you for being you. I love you," she said, a lilt in her voice, taking the arm he offered.

"Now, isn't that nice. I'm the luckiest man in the world, and you're the most devoted wife."

But Isabelle was feeling unsettled and fragile, and Lyle's words, rather than comfort, brought tears to her eyes. She brushed the tears away with her fingers, exasperated, and laughed when his expression turned serious with concern.

"Oh, bother," she said. "I didn't mean for this to happen."

Lyle rested his hand on her back and guided her further from the quarry, helping her to sit at the bench under the oak tree.

"Bella, what's troubling you?" he asked. "What's really going on?"

"I'm sorry to interrupt you at work," she said, sniffling, forcing herself under control. She looked at him and made her face stern. "But I'm so worried, I couldn't wait another minute."

Lyle took her hand and squeezed. "Is it Lavinia?"

Isabelle nodded, holding back a sob. "It's the way people talk about her. I can't bear it."

"I don't blame you for worrying, sweetheart. But people are kind to her. And their chatter isn't mean-spirited."

"They talk down to her. They patronize her. That's even worse."

Lyle sighed in understanding. There was nothing he could say.

"It's not just that, though. Have you noticed..." Isabelle began, her forehead crinkling, "anything strange going on at home?"

Lyle studied her, seeming to consider. "I don't believe I have." He paused. "Have you?"

"Yes," said Isabelle. She swallowed. "Lavinia seems...generally absent. As if she's preoccupied."

"Actually, I've found Lavinia to be quite pleasant. She always smiles, and she seems to bring happiness into every room she enters."

"That's just it," said Isabelle. "There's almost...a golden glow about her." She watched her husband carefully. "Do you follow?"

Lyle nodded, thinking. "Yes, I suppose I agree. Well said."

"No," said Isabelle. "I don't mean figuratively."

Lyle frowned. "Now I'm not sure I understand your meaning."

Isabelle sighed. "I might as well just say it straight." She fiddled with her fingers as she began. "Sometimes at night, I walk by her room. I hear Lavinia talking to herself, or sighing, or even singing. Sometimes I hear noises, too, like furniture moving, or the bed rattling. And I notice something odd. There's a light emanating from under the door, when there shouldn't be."

"I don't think there's anything odd in that. Perhaps she lit a candle so she could read."

"Perhaps. But..."

Lyle was watching her. Isabelle went on.

"I noticed it once or twice. So I've been making a point of checking every night." Isabelle's voice began to falter as she came to the most difficult part of her story. "Last night, my curiosity got the best of me. I'm ashamed to admit it. But I tiptoed toward her room and carefully opened her door."

Lyle cocked his head and frowned. "My dear. You didn't."

"I did. And what I saw, well...I don't know what to make of it."

Lyle shook his head. "You musn't tell me. It isn't—"

"Lavinia's room was flooded with light. And there was Lavinia, lying in bed—"

Lyle by now looked unsettled and disturbed. "My dear. I beg you, say no more. And leave Lavinia be. You have no right to spy on her. Whatever she must do, she must do."

"But aren't you concerned? Don't you want to know what's going on?"

"No. Most definitely, I do not."

"Why not? Isn't it odd? Aren't you worried she's a harm to herself?"

Lyle stood, and Isabelle followed. Lyle placed his hands on her shoulders and spoke to her quietly, with tenderness.

"I know how you love your sister," he said. "I know your heart is good, as are your intentions. I have no doubt there is a logical explanation for all this. If you wish to know what it is, I implore you to ask her yourself."

Isabelle sighed inwardly. She nodded. "Yes, dear," she whispered, accepting with a lift of her chin the kiss he planted delicately on her cheek.

He met her gaze and frowned. "I hope you understand. It is unbefitting for me to hear this. Already I've heard too much."

Isabelle understood, and she smiled weakly. "You are a good husband, and a good brother-in-law. And you are wise. I shall ask Lavinia herself."

They kissed again, and parted ways.

BACK HOME, Isabelle removed her cloak and hung it on the coatrack as Lavinia greeted her with a warm smile.

"I just made some tea. I'll pour you some," said Lavinia, ushering her sister in. "We have some nice tarts, too, from Mrs. Lowell. She was nice enough to drop them off today."

"Yes, I know," said Isabelle. She rubbed her arms against the chill and joined Lavinia at the back of the house in the small kitchen, instantly greeted by the pleasant warmth of the cast iron stove. "I saw her this morning. She said you were in bright spirits when she called to collect her dress."

"Well, it's a beautiful day." Lavinia took the teapot in her hand and poured tea into two floral teacups. "It's hard not to be in bright spirits today."

Isabelle watched her sister as she puttered about the room. With its uneven, cream-colored walls and scuffed hardwood floor, a single slim recessed window that, looking out into the trees, let in little light, and low, puckered ceiling, the room could have felt dank and dreary. But Lavinia had made it charming and cheerful, with woven rugs by the stove and doorway, a simple table she had painted pale blue, and a rocking chair that had belonged to their mother. A few tall iron jugs were stored beneath the table against the wall. A cuckoo clock hung above the table, beneath that a little shelf holding various knickknacks. It was these little touches that lent the room its coziness.

"It isn't seemly, Lavvy."

Lavinia turned to face her.

"Whatever do you mean?"

Isabelle's eyes turned misty with tears. "Theodore's death," she whispered, as if she couldn't bear to acknowledge it out loud. "It's been only weeks since it was confirmed. Yet you do not mourn him. You never show your grief."

"Would you prefer for me to be unhappy?"

"Well, no, of course not. But how could you be otherwise?

Lavinia stared at her for a long time. Her expression was severe, her eyes wide and alert and her lips straight. The color had drained from her face. Isabelle couldn't help being a little frightened.

"Lavvy..." she began shakily.

"I have to tell you something," said Lavinia, in a low voice her sister didn't recognize. "But you musn't tell a soul."

"Of course I won't. What is it?"

Lavinia stepped toward her sister and took her hands. "Let's sit down."

They walked back toward the front of the house and sat together on the settee. Isabelle waited while Lavinia straightened her skirts around her hips and legs, biting her lip. Finally she turned to her sister.

"Do you ever," she began hesitantly, "talk to Mother and Father?"

Isabelle was taken aback. She sat straighter, and her lips parted.

"Well, I...I suppose I do. But what does—"

"And do you ever," Lavinia went on, "believe they hear you?"

Isabelle wasn't sure what Lavinia was expecting her to say. She remained silent.

Lavinia nodded, her eyes gentle with understanding. "You

must think me mad," she said. "But I promise, I have reason to ask these questions."

"Well, for heaven's sake, Lavinia, get to the point, then."

Lavinia took a deep breath and swallowed. "What if I told you that Theodore...that Theodore is here?"

The wheels turned in Isabelle's mind, and she frowned as she realized what Lavinia was trying to tell her. Tears sprang to her eyes, and she shook her head.

"I speak the truth," said Lavinia, her hand now on her sister's knee. "Please hear what I have to say."

Isabelle was pulling a handkerchief from the pocket of her dress and wiping her nose and eyes. "Dear, sweet Lavvy," she whispered. "I know how badly you want to believe this. I understand. But—"

"No, you do not understand. Hush now."

Isabelle nodded and sniffled, looking downward, unable to meet her sister's gaze.

From above, she heard Lavinia take another breath and continue.

"Theodore has returned to me," she said. "His spirit has. And we've been living as husband and wife again, and it's been wonderful, and I've never been happier in all my life."

Isabelle closed her eyes against the tears. Already she was considering what they would do with Lavinia, how they would ensure she could take care of herself and was safe, now that she was proving to be out of her mind. Perhaps if she had a nurse, someone to watch over her—but no, they couldn't afford a nurse. Isabelle would oversee her caretaking herself. She didn't mind, really; Lavinia was her sister, and—

"Isabelle."

Lavinia's sweet voice drew her from her thoughts. She opened her eyes and looked at her sister through a cloud of tears.

"I know what you must think," Lavinia said with a sigh. "You think that I'm hysterical, that I've become delusional because I'm mad from grief. But really, I'm not. Theodore lies with me at night and rises with me in the morning. We talk as I dress and tend to the house. He keeps me company while I work and during my walks to the market. But that's not all." Lavinia leaned forward, her eyes widening and her voice growing quiet and intense. "He tells me stories of his adventures. He travels all over the world. The things he's seen, Isabelle. The beautiful things he's seen! You cannot imagine how lovely the world is, and all its different people. When it's my time, he will take me to these places so I can see them for myself. "

Isabelle watched her younger sister with sorrow. It was always so hard to resist her, with her pretty heart-shaped face and wide blue eyes. She seemed perpetually to smile, even when she was not smiling; the sweetness of her features drew one to her, made one remember the goodness in the world.

Isabelle couldn't help but smile, too. She brushed a stray tear from her cheek and nodded at her sister. Lavinia needed to feel connected to Theodore; she was not yet ready to face her husband's death. Isabelle was determined to indulge her in her need.

"All right, dear," she said, taking Lavinia's hands in her own. "Tell me what has happened."

Lavinia's smile widened with excitement. She squeezed Isabelle's hands and settled in a little closer.

"Well," she began. "It was the night of the winter solstice."

"The night we received word that the stern had washed ashore."

"Yes. I know I should have been devastated by the news. Indeed, I knew it at the time. But I simply...wasn't. I couldn't explain it. I just didn't believe Theodore was gone. As you recall, I went upstairs to bed, and you let yourself out. But what you didn't know was that when I entered my bedroom, Theodore was there, waiting for me."

Despite her skepticism, Isabelle was entranced. She listened in silence, waiting for Lavinia to continue.

"At first he was merely a presence in the room," Lavinia said. "I felt it upon entering—a happy, calm sense of peace. The room looked brighter than I had expected; it was night time, after all, and the room was glowing, as if lit from below by the flame of an enormous candle. I took a moment to enjoy this feeling. I stood inside the doorway and closed my eyes, and wrapped my arms around myself. It was then that he arrived. That he congregated."

Isabelle's breath caught. "Congregated?"

"Yes. As I stood there, eyes closed...I felt him kiss me. His soft lips on mine, so gentle. And then he parted my lips with his, and he breathed his breath into me. I gasped and opened my eyes. And there he was, Isabelle. Standing just before me. He was glowing, like the light in the room, and I knew then. I just knew."

"Were you sad, then? Were you sad that he was gone?"

"No, dear. I could feel that he was happy. You see, Isabelle," Lavinia said, and her expression turned more serious, "Theodore always wanted more. He wanted freedom to see the Earth and to explore. He always felt that he was destined to live in the stars. There was something...ethereal about him, no?"

Isabelle found herself nodding in agreement.

Encouraged, Lavinia went on. "He told me his ship had been lost at sea and that there had been no survivors. He admitted to having been frightened at the time, but said that he had been quickly overwhelmed by a sense of anticipation. He told me the water became the sky, and that before he knew it, he was among the stars, no longer drowning, but soaring high, with what he calls the particles of his spirit dispersed across the universe."

Isabelle closed her eyes and shook her head. "I'm afraid I don't understand."

"Yes, it is *so* difficult to explain!" Lavinia sighed with frustration. "The rules of the spirit are not the rules of the body. The spirit is not bound by physical restraints, you see. Theodore described it this way. He is simultaneously everywhere and nowhere. He can spread across the sky and the Earth, or he can concentrate his spirit in one place. Sometimes, Theodore chooses to dissipate the particles of his spirit to foreign places, to learn of new people and to see far off lands." Lavinia smiled. "And sometimes, he chooses to congregate the particles of his spirit around me."

"But how?" Isabelle cried, gesturing with her hands. "A person cannot fly around the world and return by morning. There's no sense in it!"

Lavinia's back straightened, and she frowned. "You don't believe me. But I tell you, it's true."

"Where is he, then? Tell him to show himself to me."

"Only I can see him. Our spirits are connected."

"What of the other men lost? Why haven't they returned?"

"Theodore thinks it's because he's always been of two worlds. And because of our connection to the solstice."

"Lavinia," said Isabelle, closing her eyes once more and holding her hands to her temples, feeling a headache coming on. She opened her eyes and firmed her face. "Isn't it possible you're imagining this?"

"No. It's definitely not possible."

"But how can you be sure?"

"Because he..."

She stopped, studying her sister.

Exasperated, Isabelle made a gasping sound with her throat. "Because he...?" she prompted, motioning with her hands for Lavinia to continue.

Lavinia was staring at her, wide-eyed, the bridge of her forehead raised with wonder and her lips parted. "Because he comes to me," she whispered. "As a husband."

Isabelle sat stunned and speechless. Understanding hit her,

and she shook her head, with a renewal of tears. "Oh, Lavinia. You poor thing. I know you can't mean—"

"But I do. And I want to tell you about it."

Isabelle sighed audibly as a desperate feeling unsettled her stomach. "If you must, but I—"

"Why wouldn't you want to hear it? It's beautiful."

Isabelle looked at Lavinia, who was sitting calmly, her eyes sparkling. Her sister's innocence, her willingness to believe her delusions to assuage her grief, touched and tormented her. She sniffled into her handkerchief.

"Go on then," she whispered, fortifying herself. "Tell me."

A little smile crept across Lavinia's sweet face. "Thank you," she said. "But first, I must ask you. What, do you think, do you love most about...about being with Lyle?"

Isabelle knew what Lavinia meant. She flushed, profoundly uncomfortable. "Oh, well...I suppose it would be...his closeness to me."

Lavinia's face brightened. "Yes," she said, her voice now intense. "Yes, I agree. The closeness to one's husband, that is the best part."

Isabelle swallowed, relieved, and fidgeted with her hands as she waited for her sister to continue.

"Now," said Lavinia, edging closer, and lowering her voice. "Imagine if a husband...if he can truly become one with you... if he can actually be a part of you."

Isabelle stared at her blankly.

Lavinia looked to the side, and her eyes turned upward as she considered what to say. "Imagine," she said, gesturing airily with her hands, "that moment, when he lowers his chest to yours, and your skin presses to his, and you feel the heat of his body, the heat he feels for you."

Isabelle's heart pounded. She could perfectly imagine this, but was loath to admit it.

Lavinia continued.

"Imagine how your cheek brushes his, and you inhale his scent, the scent of...of the forest, and of shaving soap, and of the leather of his boots."

Isabelle took a breath, imagining.

"Now imagine your arms as they wrap around his shoulders, the way your hands feel as they spread across his thick, strong back, the way his hips move, the way he moves with you..." Lavinia closed her eyes. "...The way it feels to enclose him, to be wrapped around him."

Isabelle, too, closed her eyes for a moment, resisting the urge to dab at her forehead with her handkerchief.

"Now," said Lavinia, opening her eyes and looking at her sister. "Imagine what it all would be like, if instead of above you, he lay... within you."

Despite herself, Isabelle felt drawn by Lavinia's words. She said nothing, but leaned forward expectantly.

"When Theodore comes to me...he needn't stop where I begin and he ends. He can...press himself further, and...I can feel him inside me. His heartbeat...his breath...the rushing of his blood, the thoughts in his head. I feel him, all over...the essence of his spirit...it fills me...*all* of me."

"All of you," repeated Isabelle, entranced.

Lavinia's dark eyelashes fluttered a little. "The sensation, Bella." One corner of her mouth turned up mischievously. "It's really quite astounding."

Isabelle sat back as she registered these words; unwittingly, her body responded by bristling with goosebumps. Lavinia nodded knowingly.

"You understand," she whispered, smiling.

Isabelle cleared her throat and fussed with her skirt. "Yes," she said. "I believe I do."

"But you don't believe me."

Isabelle was silent. Lavinia's smile sobered.

"I want to," said Isabelle, the honesty heavy in her voice. "I just wish there were some proof."

"Oh, but there is."

Isabelle straightened with surprise.

Without a word, Lavinia brought her slender fingers to the front of her dress, and she pressed her hands to her belly.

"What is this?" whispered Isabelle. "What do you mean to tell me?"

"I mean to tell you that it's finally happened. Theodore and I are having a child together."

Isabelle shook her head as if doing so could unsay Lavinia's words. "No. This is absurd. You cannot believe this."

"But I do believe it, because it's true. Before Theodore left, so many months went by without a child. I thought I would never be a mother, and I was devastated. Now I have my greatest wish. And I'm thrilled!"

Isabelle now understood why people in town talked to Lavinia as if she were a child playing make believe: they talked to her that way because that's exactly what she was. Isabelle loved her sister too much to have seen it before, but now she saw it all too well. As Lavinia sat there watching her—with her eyes so wide and sincere, and her lips turned up prettily—Isabelle wondered what she should do, whether she should try to force some sense into her sister—or whether she should pretend to share in her happiness, and good sense be damned.

She couldn't bring herself to shatter her sister's joy, however insane. Doing so would only make her sister feel more alone. She straightened her back and set her jaw and forced herself to smile.

"I am so happy for you, Lavvy," she said, her eyes brimming with tears, though not for that reason. "It looks like you have everything you ever wanted."

Lavinia's forehead rose, and her smile brightened; evidently she had not been expecting this reaction. She pulled her sister in for a tight embrace, and Isabelle embraced her, holding her and patting her back as she used to when they were little girls.

"Thank you for that," said Lavinia. "It means so much to me that I can share this with you. You're a good sister."

"I will always be your sister," said Isabelle, with a sigh. "And I will always love you."

CHAPTER 6

"*T*his is some story," said Nick, one arm leaning casually on the ledge behind his bench, his body relaxed as he listened. "I wasn't expecting it to go in this direction. Lavinia seemed like such a practical girl. I guess she just couldn't let go."

"*Would you?*"

Nick imagined his wife's face. He smiled solemnly. "*I guess I wouldn't.*"

"*I suspect your wife wouldn't, either.*"

Nick's expression grew sad as he imagined his wife in Lavinia's place. Only she would have their two children to comfort, too.

"So what happened?" Nick asked, changing the subject. "Did Lavinia claim to have a baby?"

"*Indeed, she did. She was quite bold about it, too, walking around town with a carriage for her ghost child, singing lullabies in her bedroom at night. Though she never talked about it, as time went on, she grew less and less inclined to hide it. Everyone knew Lavinia as the woman with the ghost family. Nobody asked questions, and nobody gave her trouble; she certainly wasn't hurting anyone. In fact, the townspeople found her extraordinary imagination delightful. It made her happy and eager to make others happy, too. She loved helping people. She cooked for the elderly, read to the schoolchildren, and sang in the town choir. All this was in addition to her sewing and her helping Isabelle around the house. She became a fixture in the town. People were used to her, and they loved her."*

"So she never backed down. Do you think she really believed it?"

"All I can say, son, is that she stuck to her story until her dying day."

THE YEARS THUS PASSED. Lavinia lived with Isabelle in the decades that followed, a beloved sister, and a beloved aunt to Betsy, who married and moved with her husband and children to a farm outside of town. After Lyle passed away, many years later, Isabelle and Lavinia lived together, just the two of them, sitting together by the hearth, their stockinged feet warming by the fire; performing charity work for the church; reading aloud to each other by lantern light, until they began dozing off.

It was a happy, serene existence. Isabelle accepted her ghostly brother-in-law and niece, whom she never saw, but frequently heard about. Isabelle indulged Lavinia, listening with interest to her tales of the places to which Theodore had taken their daughter Eugenia. Theodore and Eugenia, apparently, had visited marvelous sites all over the world, and seen all sorts of fascinating people. According to Lavinia, Theodore promised her that one day, he would take her to these places, too.

Isabelle grew to enjoy Lavinia's stories about Theodore and Eugenia. They were interesting and exciting, and full of colorful characters. She liked the way her sister's eyes gleamed, the way she felt important when she told them. Despite logic, she found herself caring about her ghostly family. Isabelle didn't understand how she had grown so fond of these invisible, imaginary people, who lived in Lavinia's head. But the years had softened her attachment to convention, and she allowed herself to be pulled into the stories' magic.

Isabelle and Lavinia grew quite old, as people tend to do. Lavinia was now frail and weary, her long dark locks scraggly and gray, and she was ready to join Theodore and Eugenia on their adventures. She took to her bed one day, resigned to never rising from it again. Isabelle sat with her tearfully, holding her hand, as the two of them remembered all the happy days of their lives.

"Theodore wants me to tell you," said Lavinia hoarsely, with the little breath she had left, "that Lyle says you look more beautiful every day."

Isabelle's heart warmed, then ached as she thought of her kind, cheerful husband. She brushed a few stray tears from her cheeks.

"Dear Bella," Lavinia went on. "I want to say thank you."

"What for?"

"For your deception."

Isabelle wrinkled her already heavily wrinkled brow. "Pardon?"

Lavinia smiled, and in that moment, Isabelle saw the sister of her youth. "My dear," she said, patting Isabelle's hand. "I know you never believed me. About Theodore."

Isabelle blanched and said nothing.

Lavinia's voice was gentle. "Do you deny it?"

Isabelle hesitated a moment, then shook her head. Her wise old eyes were clouded with tears. "I'm sorry," she whispered shakily.

"You musn't apologize."

"But I lied to you."

"You allowed me my happiness. You supported me when everyone else called me mad."

Isabelle smiled and wiped her tears with her fingers.

Lavinia was regarding her sister intently. "Even so," she said. "I spoke the truth."

The corners of Isabelle's eyes crinkled. She squeezed Lavinia's hand.

After Lavinia had taken her final breath, Isabelle began the final chapter of her own life. Her daughter Betsy helped her pack her things, so she could live out her days in Betsy's farmhouse surrounded by family. Lavinia had had few belongings, which had largely remained untouched. But on that day, Isabelle sorted through what remained—little trinket boxes, letters tied neatly with ribbons, a few frocks she had left hanging in the closet.

She came across a little jewelry box that had been given to Lavinia by their mother. The box was porcelain, painted light blue, with a medallion on top, depicting a romantic scene between a man and a woman, in which the man was handing the woman a bouquet of red flowers. Isabelle let her fingers brush across the ornate gold accents. She unhooked the clasp and lifted the lid. The box was lined with red velvet. Inside rested Lavinia's only jewelry, inherited from her mother—a pair of pearl earrings, a gold necklace, a peacock brooch with a ruby and an emerald.

Isabelle spotted in the box an item she hadn't seen in many years, not since Lavinia had shown it to her before Theodore went to sea. She pulled it from the others. It was a locket watch fob, in simple gold. She squinted to read the engraving: "TS + LL, winter solstice '56."

"How on Earth..." whispered Isabelle, her mind awhirl.

"Mother," said Betsy, entering the room, brushing off her apron with her hands. "What have you there?" she asked, noticing the object in Isabelle's hand.

Stunned, Isabelle handed it to her. Betsy took it, fondled it in her fingers for a moment, and read the inscription.

"How odd," Betsy said. "I thought Uncle Theodore took this with him when he went to sea."

"He did. Lavinia told me she gave it to him on the dock."

"But then how would Aunt Lavinia have it in her jewelry box?" She studied Isabelle's face. "Mother, you don't believe Uncle Theodore actually came home, do you?" She rested her hand gently on her mother's shoulder. "It is tempting to believe that. But—"

"No, I don't believe it," said Isabelle wistfully, her eyes distant. "I suppose there must be a reasonable explanation for this."

Betsy kissed her mother's cheek and carried some blankets out of the room, leaving Isabelle alone.

For the rest of her days, Isabelle lived peacefully in her daughter's farmhouse, enjoying the company of her grandchildren and the comforting routines of the farm. Somehow, her world had been brightened when she found that locket. In her mind, she believed, as she always had, that Lavinia had invented her life with Theodore. But part of her, in the very deepest recesses of her heart, was eager for the day when she would see her husband again, when she would visit all the magical places of Lavinia's stories, when she would have her own adventures.

～

"*WHEW,*" *said Nick with a laugh, leaning back against his seat and folding his arms across his chest.* "*That was some story.*"

"*You liked it?*"

"*Sure I did. I've lived here for years, but I'd never heard anything about Lavinia or her family. I like hearing the local lore. I love it here. I think these stories are part of the town's character.*"

"*You're right, son. They give the town its charm, much like Lavinia did.*"

"*So does Isabelle's family still live here?*"

"*No, they didn't stay here. The grandkids sold the farm and scattered across the country. But Lavinia's family comes back here occasionally.*"

"*Lavinia's family,*" *Nick repeated. His brow furrowed. He leaned forward, folded his hands on the table, and watched the flame of the candle that burned in its globe-shaped holder between them.* "*Wait a second. There's something I don't understand. If Lavinia and Theodore never had any children, then how did you—*"

Nick looked up with a start. His heart jumped: the man in brown had disappeared.

He stood abruptly and looked around, his face taut. He moved with long strides out from behind the table and searched the bar, but the man in brown was nowhere to be found.

The door opened, the wind blowing gusts of snow inside. Nick turned toward the door, expecting, hoping, to see the man in brown. But it was only Nick's brother-in-law Vince, bundled up in his winter gear. Nick watched distractedly as Vince unraveled himself, first removing his gloves, then his scarf, then his hat, revealing a head of fashionably spiked chocolate brown hair.

"Holy hell, it's cold," Vince said, rubbing his hands together and shivering in an exaggerated manner. "I don't think I'll ever get used to this."

Nick stood still in the middle of the room, his eyes wide. He looked around again, back and forth, searching.

"Hey man, sorry I'm late," said Vince as he approached. His cheeks were red with cold. He smacked the sides of his coat to remove some snow. "You still want to grab a beer, or what?"

Nick ran his fingers through his hair and frowned. "I don't know. I..."

"Hey, you okay? You look spooked."

Nick looked at Vince, who was standing there casually, infuriatingly calm, with his hands shoved into the pockets of his jeans. Vince then slapped him on the back. "Long day, huh? Looks like you need that beer more that I thought."

Nick swallowed and glanced over his shoulder as Vince tried to draw him toward a table.

"So what's happening?" asked Vince, removing his coat and throwing it askance on the back of a chair. He sat down heavily, then pushed up the sleeves of his black sweater. "What did you want to talk to me about?"

Nick remained standing. "Hey, have you ever heard of Lavinia Lockett Sewall?"

"Who the hell is Lavinia Lockett Sewall?"

"Or her husband Theodore?"

"No. Is he a potential client?"

Nick's eyes took in the sight of his brother-in-law, with his carefree smile, warm brown eyes, and slick black clothing. The two couldn't have been more different. Nick was from a small town. Pensive and soft-spoken, he loved where he lived, with its dense forests and rugged shorelines, and he spent his spare time outdoors with his wife and children. Vince was stylish and urbane, and while he adored his own wife and daughter, he had settled down by accident, his past littered with devilry. But somehow, the friendship between them worked. They had had ups and downs together, had known each other for many years and had built a relationship that respected the strengths of each, and forgave the weaknesses. They had in common a mutual devotion to Nick's wife, who was Vince's sister, and they had made the welfare and happiness of their extended family the shared purpose of their lives.

Suddenly Nick couldn't bring himself to have the conversation he had brought Vince here to have. He didn't want to disappoint him or to travel far from his family. He didn't want to prioritize money over the people he cared most about in the world. He didn't want to change his situation; he was fortunate to have it.

"I think I'm going to go home," he told Vince. "It's late. I want to see Merry."

"Merry'll be there in an hour. Come on, sit down. Let's shoot the bull for a while."

Nick stepped toward the table but didn't sit. "Listen," he said. "I just want to tell you what a good guy you are. I don't tell you that enough." He paused, collecting himself. "You're a good friend."

Vince's face creased between the eyes, then softened. He stood to face Nick.

"Thanks, man," he said, his voice unusually gentle. "I appreciate that. The feeling's mutual." His expression turned questioning. "You sure you're okay?"

"I'm great," said Nick, bringing Vince in for a firm hug. He patted him on the back. "I'll see you tomorrow."

Vince reciprocated the hug. "Sure. Let's get out of here."

Nick tossed a bill in the jar at the bar and walked with Vince out into the cold.

~

"HONEY," *Nick whispered as he lay on his side in bed, smoothing back his wife's chestnut hair. "Honey, wake up."*

Meredith stirred, then opened her eyes and squinted into the darkness. She smiled when she saw his face hovering just above hers. "Hi," she said groggily, stretching a little. "Did you just get home?"

Nick nodded, a soft smile on his lips, warmth filling him.

"Did you talk to him?"

Nick shook his head. "No."

Meredith opened her eyes wider, now fully awake. "You didn't? Why not?"

His fingers stroked the side of her face. "I changed my mind about the job."

Her eyelashes fluttered a couple of times at the tender touch of his fingers. She looked at him quizzically. "What brought this on?"

He brushed his finger over the corner of her lips, which were curved into a little smile. It was so good to come home to her after a long day, to see her pretty face and to be reminded of all the reasons he loved her. "I was just thinking of you, and the kids..." He sighed and shrugged. "You know, the job seemed like the sensible thing to do, but for some reason, it never really felt right." His eyes turned serious. "What do you think?"

She brought her hand to his and held it as it cupped her face, and the comforting warmth made his heart lurch. "I know it's a great opportunity, and you should have it if that's what you want. But if it were up to me..." She squeezed his hand, and her smile grew wider. "I feel the same way. I want you home."

He leaned in farther and kissed her. Her hand went to the back of his head, her other hand around his neck. He buried his fingers in her hair, his thumb brushing against her temple. She arched her body toward him, and he let his hand drift over her back and around the curve of her hip. He deepened the kiss, his heart beginning to pound at the promise of her skin beneath her nightgown and the soft sigh that rose from her throat.

"I love you," he murmured into her ear, his hand splayed across her lower back and pulling her in close.

"I love you too, honey." She opened her eyes and looked into his. "Did something happen tonight?"

"I don't know. It's kind of hard to explain."

"Do you want to talk about it?"

"Maybe in the morning," he said, his voice trailing off as his lips traveled up her neck. "I've had my fill of talking tonight."

She smiled and slid her arms around him, her chin lifting to meet his kiss as he shifted on top of her, the darkness made silver by the moonlight streaming in through the window. Outside, a brisk breeze wafted through the trees like spirits, and the stars glittered and sparkled, making the sky appear to undulate like a tranquil sea.

THE END

MEREDITH OUT OF THE DARKNESS

She's created the perfect life. But when it doesn't turn out as planned, can she take what she's learned and find her way in the darkness?

Meredith Beck had it all: the love of her life, a thriving career, and an apartment in the excitement of New York City. Then tragedy strikes, leaving her adrift in a world that's suddenly lost its luster. Optimistic by nature, she desperately attempts to rebuild. But no matter how hard she tries, she just can't muster her former strength.

Then a light appears in the darkness: Nick Kelly, a quiet painter from a small town in Maine. Thoughtful and kind, and utterly without pretension, Nick is unlike anyone Meredith has ever known. She is drawn to his love of nature and is comforted by his purity of heart. Through his eyes, the world seems to hold limitless possibility, and as their romance blossoms, she's delighted to find herself on the road toward a simpler life, with a partner who reminds her of the beauty in every moment.

But it isn't as simple as it seems. As Nick's own demons surface, the life they're building threatens to unravel. Human fallibilities once again complicate best-laid plans. And it becomes clear that before they can embrace the future, they must confront the lingering ghosts of their pasts.

A story of love, loss, and the power of second chances, *Meredith Out of the Darkness* is first in a slow-burn series of cliffhangers ending with a warm and satisfying happily-ever-after.

ALSO BY AMANDA GALE

Meredith Out of the Darkness

Meredith Against the Wind

Meredith Into the Fire

Meredith With the Waves

Strawberry and Sage

Love in the Lavender

Catherine and the Wind

Gwyneth in the Garden

Maeve in the Morning

The Magic You Bring

Dahlia Almost Drowning

ACKNOWLEDGMENTS

Thank you to those who graciously helped me make *Sweet Lavvy* a reality: Judy, Melissa, Jessica, George, Terri, Cindy, Tammy, Sara, Jennifer, Rachel, April, Bryn, G. G., and Saskia.

An extra special thank you to historian Melanie Stringer, whose knowledge and guidance were invaluable as I worked to write dialogue appropriate for the 19th century, fine tune details of the characters' daily lives, and recreate as historically accurate a world as possible. In a couple of instances, I made editorial choices in favor of the storytelling. Any fanciful deviations are fully my own.